Merry Christmas 2010 Christine & Gary.
Hope this book either resides at
your Hideaway, or at least helps
bring your thoughts there when
away!
Love Charles & Cynthia

Tales of St. John
and the Caribbean

Collected by Gerald Singer

Printed in the United States of America
Library of Congress Control Number 00-136279
ISBN #0-9641220-2-2

Compiled by Gerald Singer
Edited by Connie MacNamee

Cover Art by David Wegman
Graphic Design by Michael Barry, Dawgs of St. John Inc.
Printed by Book-mart Press

SOMBRERO PUBLISHING COMPANY
P.O. Box 1031
St. John, United States Virgin Islands, 00831-1031

e-mail: gsinger@islands.vi

TABLE OF CONTENTS

ACKNOWLEDGEMENTS

Most of these stories first appeared on the back page of the St. John newspaper, *Tradewinds,* as an ad for Marina Market. The page was paid for by the market's owner Michaela "Mimi" Alioto. When I asked Mimi why she chose to run my stories instead of using more conventional advertising, she answered by saying, "That's what Marina Market is all about." Behind that somewhat enigmatic response is the fact that to Mimi, Marina Market is not just a business, it's her way of being an integral part of the St. John community, and, using Marina Market as a vehicle, she happily and unselfishly shares her time and resources with the people of her adopted home.

Connie MacNamee is an editor, proofreader and jazz singer, but really she's some sort of angel. Connie has an aura about her that glows like sunlight, warming everyone who's fortunate enough to come in contact with her. Every editing session left me with a renewed feeling of enthusiasm and excitement about the book project, about the island of St. John, and about life in general.

Connie, I cannot thank you enough.

A journey of a thousand miles starts with the first step. That first step, however, is a scary one to take. It was Constance Wallace who encouraged me to make that quantum leap. Constance happens to be an excellent writer in addition to her better-known talents in the world of business and photography. She took time out of her busy schedule to work with me on several of these stories, when they were Marina Market ads or newspaper articles and, in the process, helped me to sharpen my writing skills and learn to focus on a goal. Now when I reread my material, I always recognize those sentences and phrases that came from Constance. They are invariably the best and most witty ones in the whole story.

Constance is a gem!

Besides Connie and Constance, there were others who reviewed, edited and proofread. When I first arranged the Marina Market ads and *Tradewinds* articles into book form, the collection was reviewed and edited by the charming Sonja Tuffli and my lovely sister, Ellen.

Kathleen Brennan was a great help and proved to be a fine editor to boot, bringing back to life a particularly good story that I was about to give up on.

As the book evolved and other authors came onboard, I often found myself calling on those close to me when I needed help, opinions, advice or moral support; among whom are:

Art "Art the Painter" Albricht, Hyacinth Ashley, Emanuel "Mano" Boyd (my biggest fan on St. John), Foxy and Tessa Callwood, Sid Carter, Tal Carter, Ivan Chinnery, Charles "Trinidad Charlie" Deyalsingh, Brian Hadley, John and Teri Gibney, Mario "Chin" Jackson, Wilmoth King, Peter Laurincin, Mervin form Dominica, Brion Morrisette, Delbert Parsons, Ralph Powell, Laura and Paul "Ras Paul" Samm, Ray Samuels, Dan Silber, Hermon Smith and Dr. Robert Walker.

My son Sean served as the critic. He would read whatever I had for him while on his way to work aboard the "N" train in New York City and then (candidly) let me know when I needed to do a better job, give up on weak material or start all over again on a story that I had been working on for days. It was an unenviable job that he performed admirably. Thanks, kid.

Setting the tone for the stories is the artwork on the cover of the book, which was suggested by the aforementioned Constance Wallace. The cover art was reproduced from the original oil painting, *Out Where the Busses Don't Run*, by that incredible artist and Caribbean character's character, David Wegman. The design work was courtesy of my favorite graphic designer, restaurateur, and all-around good guy, Michael Barry.

Last, but certainly not least, I wish to express my heartfelt appreciation to the authors who contributed their stories to this book – Jack Andrews, Curtney "Ghost" Chinnery, John Gibney, Andrew Rutnik and Bob Tis.

THE WELL-KNOWN SAILOR

By Gerald Singer

The Tomb of the Unknown Soldier in Arlington, Virginia, is a memorial to those soldiers who have lost their lives in war, but whose bodies were unrecognizable or have never been found. On the island of St. Barths, there is a similar memorial dedicated to sailors. This one commemorates not only those whose bodies have never been found, but also the departed souls of all sailors, everywhere. It is called the Tomb of the Well-Known Sailor and was conceived of by David Wegman, the artist whose painting, *Out Where the Busses Don't Run*, appears on the cover of this book.

In addition to being an artist, Wegman is himself a sailor, fiddle player, singer, storyteller and undoubtedly much more. He travels extensively, spending most of his time living aboard his black-hulled wooden schooner, *The Afrigan Queen*, which was built on St. John.

Wegman came to the Caribbean in the late sixties, before the islands had been discovered by mainstream yachtsmen. He joined a tightly knit group of young adventurers who sailed older wooden boats and made do however they could. Many of them were artists, musicians and writers. They shared a common sense of adventure, spirit of freedom, and love of the sea.

In 1987, David Wegman set sail from St. John en route to St. Barths in the French West Indies. It was the first leg of an around-the-world journey that gained for *The Afrigan Queen* the honor of being the only vessel ever built on St. John to circumnavigate the globe.

Upon arriving in St. Barths, Wegman's first stop was Le Select, an establishment famous within the sailing world. Here he knew that he could get in touch with his friends, pick up any messages, and hear the latest news and stories.

> *Recalling his first trip to St. Barths, Jimmy Buffett was heard to say, "When I was heading down here for the first time, and I was on my boat, I was asking about St. Barths, and someone just said: 'Find Le Select, everything will work out from there.'"*

A few days before Wegman's arrival, the bartender at Le Select had received a fax from a sailor known as Scrimshaw Mike. The message contained the upsetting news that Kenny, an old buddy of Wegman's, had died in Antigua.

Kenny was a notorious island character and modern-day pirate. Rumor had it that he had been one of those Caribbean captains involved in marijuana smuggling back in the days when drug runners were considered culture heroes. Wegman once mentioned that he knew of several sailors who "went from rice and beans to Dom Perignon overnight."

> *Son of a gun, load the last ton*
> *One step ahead of the jailer...*
> Son of a Son of a Sailor, *Jimmy Buffett*

According to another rumor, St. Martin customs officers once discovered $100,000 in cash in a briefcase that Kenny was carrying. Somehow, he was able to provide a plausible explanation and the matter never proceeded any further. There was also the story that he was arrested in Puerto Rico after a daring attempt to escape, literally running down the streets of Old San Juan with United States marshals in hot pursuit.

Kenny kept late hours and liked to party. He associated with fast-moving crowds, jet-setters and "beautiful people."

While only in his forties, Kenny developed heart problems. Nonetheless, he did not slow down. One night, on the island of Antigua in the British West Indies, Kenny joined a contingent of rock stars and their entourage for a long night of debauchery, after which he returned to his boat, which was anchored in the bay. The morning sunrise found Kenny dead in his cabin.

Wegman passed along the sad news of Kenny's demise to friends on St. Barths, such as John Smith of the Mermaid of Carriacou and Speedy John of the Gaucho.

The burial at sea was to take place off Antigua in two days.

Feeling the need to pay their last respects, a few of Kenny's old comrades made hasty preparations and set sail for Antigua.

It was a voyage that was never completed. Between St. Barths and Antigua that week were approximately 100 miles of strong headwinds and high seas. After a full day of beating against the intensified trades, called the Christmas Winds, and hardly making any progress, Kenny's buddies and cohorts realized that they would not be able to attend the funeral. Reluctantly, they turned around. Running before the wind, they sailed back to St. Barths and Le Select.

Meanwhile back in Antigua, Kenny's buddy, Roy, volunteered the use of his boat, *Sorcerer*, to carry his deceased friend out to the deep waters of the Atlantic, where his body would be committed to the sea.

In most burials at sea, the body is simply wrapped in a sail and weighed down with chains. Regulations in Antigua, for some reason, demand that the body be placed in a wooden box with holes cut out to allow water to enter. Kenny was placed in such a box, which was weighed down with stones. After a brief and touching memorial service, Kenny was cast into the ocean that had been such a great part of his life.

But Kenny was not quite ready for a final goodbye. His coffin sank below the surface of the water, but in less than one minute, it floated back up to the top.

Roy got into the dinghy, overtook the floating coffin, and secured a length of chain around the outside. The coffin once again disappeared beneath the waves.

Ten days later, back in the French West Indies, Wegman overheard some fishermen describing a macabre incident. While they had been returning to port from a day's outing, a flock of birds circling about and diving into the sea had attracted their attention. Because this is generally an indication of good fishing, they went over to investigate. When they got there, they saw that the birds were flying around a barely floating box. They brought the box alongside their boat.

The box had holes cut out in it. When the fishermen peered inside, they beheld a pale-white, bloated body. Horrified, they pushed the box away from their boat and hurriedly continued upon their way.

From the description of the box and the timing of the find, it seemed possible that the occupant inside may have been Kenny. Wegman searched the area described by the fishermen. He even circled the island in a small boat, but he didn't find anything. The next day, however, he heard that the Fire Department had found a body washed up on a nearby beach.

Wegman called the Fire Department and relayed his suspicion that the washed-up body might be that of his friend who had been buried at sea. The St. Barths' officials notified the Antiguan officials, and through the miracle of modern forensics, they were able to identify the badly decomposed body. It was Kenny!

So it came to pass that David Wegman, along with Kenny's other friends, arranged to provide him with a more secure and permanent burial, this time in a cemetery on dry land on the beautiful Caribbean island of St. Barths. The ceremony happened to take place on Easter Sunday.

Kenny would have appreciated the fact that a Heineken carton was chosen as the form to pour his concrete headstone, inscribed with Kenny's name and decorated with shells, stones and pieces of colored glass. A small brass mermaid, sculpted by Wegman, was imbedded in the center.

Soon after the burial, Wegman sailed off to the east on his extended around-the-world odyssey.

Ten years later, he returned to St. Barths. One of the items on Wegman's agenda was to visit the grave of his friend. He had difficulty finding it, because tall grass and bush had grown up around the marker.

Back at Le Select, Wegman mentioned the condition of Kenny's grave. He was told that he was lucky to have found the grave at all, because the caretakers of the cemetery would sometimes make use of untended gravesites for new burials.

Wegman and several friends on St. Barths decided to clean up the area around Kenny's grave and construct a more visible marker. They also had to come up with a program of maintenance to insure that Kenny would remain undisturbed.

With that idea in mind, the sailors at Le Select chipped in for the soon-to-be-renovated gravesite.

When the materials arrived, a friend drove Wegman to the cemetery in the morning and promised to return for him later on in the afternoon. Coincidentally, it was Easter Sunday, the tenth anniversary of Kenny's second burial.

Wegman reminded his friend to come back for him early so

that he would have time enough to get ready for the big Easter party that was scheduled for that evening.

Wegman's first task was to clear away the weeds that had grown up around Kenny's grave. He was down on his hands and knees, pulling out clumps of tall grass near the grave marker, when he noticed an odd off-white object protruding through the surface of the now-exposed earth. As he removed the soil from around the strange object, he soon realized what he had found. It was a skull!

Wegman pulled out more grass and dug a little deeper. He found an arm bone and then more bones. Had Kenny come up again?

When his friend arrived at the cemetery to pick him up, Wegman asked if it would be all right to bring someone to the party.

"Who?" inquired Wegman's buddy.

"Kenny!" he replied, displaying the newly uncovered skull. "He traveled a hundred miles from Antigua by sea and now he's come up through six feet of earth. I think the man needs a party."

"How do you know that's Kenny?" asked the friend. "That could be anybody."

"I don't know, but I think it is." Wegman replied.

At the Easter party, Kenny's friends discussed what to do with the bones, which most of them believed belonged to Kenny.

They thought about reburying them in the same grave. They also contemplated another burial at sea. None of these options especially appealed to them, because it seemed that Kenny himself might not have been happy with these resting places, given his propensity to reappear unexpectedly every so often.

It was Wegman who came up with the idea that seemed most appropriate to this gathering of sailors.

Still fresh in everyone's memory was the fate of their friend Roy, the skipper of the *Sorcerer*, who had provided the transportation for Kenny's first burial. Roy and his girlfriend had been on their way to Cuba when Roy disappeared one night during his watch. Roy's body was never found.

Kenny's grave in St. Barths is now marked by a beautiful old wooden crucifix, found in a pile of debris that had been taken from untended burial sites. Those who have lost a friend or relative to the sea are invited to carve the name of the departed into the cross. The memorial is called the Tomb of the Well-Known Sailor.

The bones from the cemetery are now aboard Wegman's black-hulled schooner. They are artfully displayed on a piece of driftwood and are destined to go to the Blue Marlin Bar in Charleston, South Carolina, a drinking establishment and gathering place in many ways similar to Le Select in St. Barth. Here Kenny's bones will repose majestically in a place of honor.

We can only assume that any element of Kenny's spirit still remaining in the DNA of his bones will be delighted to be a

Photo by Gerald Singer and Kathleen Brennan

part of the bar proceedings. And that the patrons of the Blue Marlin will undoubtedly be proud to have such an illustrious and distinguished Caribbean character in their midst.

A collection box will be placed beneath the bones to receive donations to maintain Kenny's gravesite and to buy refreshments for the annual Easter Sunday Memorial Service. This ceremony will be held for all the unknown sailors who have been lost at sea and whose bodies were never found, as well as in honor of Kenny, the Well-Known Sailor, whose body was found, again and again.

A SUNDAY MORNING SEA BREEZE STORY

BY GERALD SINGER

Trinidad Charlie and I arrived at the Sea Breeze, a popular Coral Bay hangout that served a good Sunday brunch. The Sea Breeze has since closed its doors and is no longer in operation.

We arrived about 8:30 one Sunday morning. As we were waiting around for breakfast to be served, the place began filling up with all kinds of salty characters: early morning drinkers, sailors, Coral Bay locals, and the occasional tourist.

Charlie and I struck up a conversation with a man who was sitting at the table next to us. In the course of the conversation, he told us the following story:

He had sailed out of St. Thomas on his way to the Azores. He was all alone; single-handing a wooden sloop which, although quite old, still appeared to be in excellent condition.

Riding the tradewinds, he first sailed to the northwest in order to reach the latitudes of the prevailing westerlies, which would then carry him east across the Atlantic.

He was about 100 miles north of the Turks and Caicos, and it was clear sailing with calm seas, steady winds and fine weather.

He calculated his position and determined that he was far from any recognized shipping lanes, land, shallow reefs, or other navigational hazards. The sails were well set, the tiller was lashed down and the boat was heading north, northwest with no problems. He decided it would be safe to go below and take a nap.

He awoke in the night to find the cabin awash with water. He rushed topside only to find that the seas were coming over the main deck, and it was obvious that the vessel was rapidly sinking.

What happened? He doesn't know. Perhaps a main plank had come loose, but whatever it was, there was no time to do anything but abandon ship and avoid being trapped below in the cabin.

No time to radio an SOS. He donned an ocean life vest and jumped overboard.

He watched by the light of the moon as the boat sailed gracefully on into the night under full sail. It traveled about another 100 yards before descending beneath the waves. The batteries were still functioning, and he could see the running lights and the cabin lights shining surreally under the water as the boat slowly sank.

His class-three life jacket, designed to hold a person's head above water even if they were unconscious, was equipped with a flashlight, a whistle and an emergency radio beacon, none of which was very helpful so far from any land or commercial activity.

Realizing his position, alone in the dark of night in the middle of the ocean, he thought about death and drowning and sharks. He said he felt like a piece of bait at the end of a fishing line.

Overwhelmed by fear and panic, he passed out.

He regained consciousness in the light of the next morning. He heard a sound; and then he saw God – coming down from the sky – on a rope!

"God" turned out to be a U.S. Coast Guard lieutenant.

A Coast Guard helicopter had just happened to be in the area on an unusual mission. Unusual, because flights were rarely scheduled so far from the helicopter's base of operations.

The crew had just been at the point of turning back when they had heard the faint signal of the emergency beacon.

There was scarcely enough fuel to return to base, and there was only a short amount of time for a search-and-rescue mission; but, against all odds, the Coast Guard team managed

to find and rescue the sailor and make a safe return to the
U.S. military base in Guantanamo Bay, Cuba.

He says that he still sails, but only on perfect days, when there
is not a cloud in the sky, and never very far from the sight of
land.

THE DONKEY FOOT WOMAN

By Gerald Singer

I first met Mervin when I lived in St. Thomas in the late 1960s. I had only been living in the Virgin Islands for about a month and the Caribbean experience was new and exciting. I had just purchased a 17-foot fishing boat from a Frenchtown fisherman. It was tied up to the seawall on the waterfront at Charlotte Amalie and I was standing there, looking out over the harbor, lost in daydreams about all the new adventures that awaited me. It was a feeling similar to the one I had when I bought my first automobile: a sense of freedom, of being able to get up and go wherever and whenever I wanted.

My attention was drawn to the entrance of Charlotte Amalie Harbor where a black-hulled, gaff-rigged, wooden schooner was coming in with all sails flying. I watched as the crew took down the sails and motored over to the seawall, tying up right behind my new boat.

I could see three young men standing on deck, one black and two white. They scurried about the vessel, neatly arranging the lines and sails and making everything shipshape.

The schooner carried a cargo of colorful and delicious-looking tropical fruits and vegetables from Dominica, which the crew began to organize so that they could sell them to the shoppers and passers-by on the bustling St. Thomas waterfront.

It was truly a sight to behold, especially to an American recently arrived in the Caribbean. There were mangos of all sizes and colors, bananas with names like fig, apple and horse; limes the size of melons, ugli fruit, sweet green oranges and grapefruit, small ripe pineapples, green coconuts called jelly nuts, breadfruit, papaya, star-shaped carambolas, sugar apples and soursop, colorful sweet and hot peppers, tomatoes, eggplant; and root vegetables like yam, sweet potato, tanya, yucca and boniato.

While the three young men were getting ready for the day's activities, I struck up a conversation with them, asking all kinds of questions like: What are your names? Where are you all from? What are those fruits over there? and Can I see the inside of the boat?

The two white men were British expatriates who had recently bought the old schooner for a song, but had spent a good deal of time and money in restoration and refitting. This was their first voyage of a commercial nature and all had gone well so far.

The black man was Mervin, a native of the island of Dominica. Mervin was the invaluable crewman. In addition to being a great sailor, Mervin could also be a navigator, carpenter, plumber, electrician, rigger and cook.

The schooner from Dominica was not the only boat to have brought tropical fruits and vegetables to St. Thomas. There were other boats tied up to the seawall with produce for sale from Santo Domingo, from Puerto Rico and from the British Virgin Islands. In addition, there were kiosks on the walkway that were supplied daily with fruit and vegetables brought in by air from San Juan.

Notwithstanding, the tropical produce grown in the lush volcanic soil of the Dominican mountain valleys was bigger and better and less expensive.

Although sales were brisk and steady, the young entrepreneurs decided to expand the scope of their market and came up with a more direct sales approach; one that they hoped would enable them to sell out faster, with less competition, and at higher prices. Their idea was to sell door-to-door, so to speak, stopping alongside the yachts that were anchored in the harbor or tied up at the dock at the then-prestigious Yacht Haven Marina.

To put the plan into effect, they needed a boat about the size of mine. Their schooner was too big and not maneuverable enough for such an activity, and their dinghy was too small to carry an appreciable amount of goods.

The captain made me an offer: a portion of the profits in exchange for my time and for the use of my boat. I readily accepted their proposal, delighted by the opportunity to be part of this Virgin Island adventure.

That very afternoon, when business began to slow down at the waterfront, we loaded up my boat and motored around the harbor, stopping alongside the anchored yachts to show the people our fruits and vegetables. It was an easy sell. Everything looked just too delicious to pass up.

After that day, we all stayed in touch and whenever the fruit boat was in port, we would get together socially for a drink or a night on the town.

One day after I had moved to St. John, I received a call from Mervin, who had decided to leave the fruit boat and seek his fortune in the Virgin Islands. He needed a place to stay while he was waiting to receive some documents regarding his immigration status, and I told him that he could use my apartment in Coral Bay.

As usual, Mervin proved to be helpful and multitalented. He helped me build fish traps and, in a flamboyant spectacle of religion and theater, he fortified the house against evil spirits. Carrying a coal pot full of smoldering branches, leaves and herbs into every nook and cranny of the house, he chased away any "jumbies" that might have been lurking about.

In the mornings, we went into the bush to cut birch sticks for the fish pot braces, and after lunch, we spent long and tedious hours in the front yard tying up the chicken wire traps.

In the evenings, Mervin would captivate me with stories about the wonders of Dominica: rich jungles where every kind of tropical fruit imaginable grew in abundance, haunted mountains that rose above the clouds and where the Devil himself was known to walk, spectacular waterfalls possessed with spiritual powers, and hot springs whose waters could cure illnesses and restore lost youth. He told me of trained monkeys that would climb the tall coconut trees and throw coconuts down to the gatherers below, about his maternal grandmother who was a full-blooded Carib, and a princess among her people, about magic and jumbies and ghosts and zombies who roamed about on full-moon nights in a netherworld hovering between life and death, and about the poor farmer who shared his meager plate of food with a stray mongrel dog and awoke the next morning to find a $100 bill in the gourd where he had placed the dog's food.

One story that particularly impressed me was the tale of the Donkey Foot Woman, which Mervin told me by candlelight one night when we were temporarily without electricity:

One evening, there was a festival in Mervin's village. Housewives prepared plates of fish and meats and vegetables. Others brought rum and beer. A huge bonfire lit up the clear Caribbean night and the sound of music and laughter echoed throughout the village.

At one point, a crowd drew around to observe a group of young men and women who were dancing to an ancient African rhythm, expertly played on a variety of homemade percussion instruments.

One of the dancers was not from the village. She was a beautiful white woman wearing a large straw hat. No one knew who she was or where she came from.

A little boy stood next to his mother in the crowd. He stared at the strange woman, fascinated by the spectacle and the hypnotic beat of the music. Suddenly he turned to his mother and said, "Mommy, look de woman. She have a donkey foot!"

The little boy's mother answered, "Me son, I see no woman with donkey foot."

"Momma, momma, yes, look!" the boy cried, then loud enough for all to hear he yelled, "Watch de donkey foot!"

An instant later, the little boy fell to the ground dead, his skull mashed in by a mysterious and powerful blow.

Many years have now passed and much has changed since I last saw Mervin, but I still carry fond memories of him and of those wonderful and exciting days of my initiation into the island experience.

AUTHOR'S NOTE:

My friend, John Gibney, told me that he ran into Mervin some years ago in Dominica, and that he had long dreadlocks and had adopted the Rastafarian religion and philosophy.

THE QUEEN'S PANTY

By Curtney Chinnery

In the mid-sixties, the Queen of England paid a visit to the island of Tortola. This particular story is one that probably should not be told. But what the hell, we were just children.

Let me start with the day before the Queen came to Roadtown, Tortola. There were four of us. We were called "Water Rats." There were two police officers that were assigned to the waterfront area. One of the officers called out to us saying: "Hey! Come here. Tomorrow the Queen will be here, and we don't want you Water Rats in the water. Don't let us have to chase you guys around."

Those officers were men we respected. Therefore, we promised not to be in the water. We had intentions of making good money that day from visiting tourists by diving for coins. Being that our plans were changed because of our promise, we were left with nothing in mind to do for the day of the Queen's visit. The eldest of our group, a fellow we called Hookadoe, who is no longer with us in life today, said, "I know what we can do tomorrow. Let's come early in the morning and go up under the stage."

My brother Abraham asked Hookadoe, "Why?"

"To see what color panty she'll be wearing," Hookadoe replied.

Suddenly, we all thought it was a great idea, for it meant to us that we would be the only ones who would have the pleasure of seeing the Queen's panty.

Early the following morning, Hookadoe, Abraham, our friend Blackbird and I met up at the Market Square near the waterfront. Slightly before daybreak, we made our way over the hill so that we would not be seen by anyone.

Directly above the Roadtown Post Office was an old pirates' castle, which today is the Dr. Tattersol Hospital. Sticking out from various points of the castle were heavy iron cannons pointed out towards the Roadtown harbor. There was one particular cannon we kids used to descend downwards into one of the many genip trees to get to the street below on the side of the Post Office. As we got to the street level, which is the same narrow Main Street of today, I was sent out as a scout to see if anyone was in the street.

After seeing no one, I signaled to the others to follow.

In those days, we had a wooden dock that was for ferry and

yacht discharge only. The dock directly across from the passenger dock was for cargo boats to unload. For the Queen's comfort, they constructed a large stage between both docks using many strips of wood for the floor, which made us think we would be able to look up between the many single strips of board.

We all took turns inching our way out toward the customs building at the dock. Upon arrival, we went into the water, clothes and all. The back end of the stage that faced the water was open so that we Water Rats could climb out of the water and go up under the stage.

After we made it under the stage, we undressed and wrang out our clothes. We depended upon our body heat as a drying agent to dry our clothes.

It wasn't long before people started to gather. Suddenly we heard the sound of an engine. A few moments later, two U-boats came and tied up at the end of both docks, which meant we were totally trapped. To keep from being seen we now had to move toward the front section of the stage and in our little peeping plot, there was no turning back.

That morning we had no breakfast, which was a big mistake. The crowd started to build, and beneath the stage started to get hot from the sun. There was nothing we could do but lay on the ground for a few hours. As time went by, we developed hunger. What made matters worse was the odor of fried chicken, which was causing a big problem for us.

As the hours passed, the heat built up. Our wet clothes never got a chance to dry from our body heat, because our bodies were just pushing out more water from sweat. Therefore what we did was remove our clothes.

I can remember starting to say a prayer, a prayer asking God to send the Queen soon, so that we could get out of there. There were only two ways out. One was to give up our quest. The other was to wait it out until the Queen arrived, made her speech, and moved on up through Main Street to the school-yard where many people were gathered to see her. The choice of giving up was out of the question, so we stuck it out.

As we lay upon our clothes, up under the hot darkened stage, we heard clapping through the cracks of the stage steps. I could see the crowd moving to the left side in front of the stage. This cheering, clapping, and movement of the crowd told us our big moment was about to come. We made our move to the center of the stage, so that we could have a clear view of the Queen. We all laid side by side in the area where the Queen was about to walk up on the stage.

I can remember that our hunger had intensified so much so that our stomachs were making noises. This was another problem, because the moving gas in our stomachs was loud enough to be heard from the outside. Then as we lay there trying to quiet our stomachs by squeezing them with our hands, it suddenly got very dark.

It seems that someone had just unrolled a three-foot-wide red carpet for the Queen to walk on, which posed another problem. To combat this new dilemma, my brother and I moved to one side of the carpet and Blackbird and Hookadoe the other. That way we could still view the Queen from the sides of the carpet.

The white convertible carrying the Queen drove up in front and stopped directly at the beginning of the red carpet. The car door was opened by one of our local police officers. We could now clearly see her face. Her beauty glittered as the sunlight hit her overall structure. Her large white dress was whiter than white itself. But our viewing of her was just for a brief moment. Once she came to the first step we beneath lost visual of her face.

Our big moment had finally arrived. We moved back from under the step section in an attempt to follow her movements as she was being escorted to her area upon the stage. We tried to look and peep through the cracks of the strips of wood on the sides of the carpet, except that fate was not on our side. The panty we had tried to see, for us, did not exist. All that we saw from our angle was layers and layers of material. It seems that the Queen had on about 25 dresses, one dress on top of another. We did not even get to see her ankle. The only part of her skin we saw was what all had seen, which was from her elbow to below her shoulders and her face. All other parts of her body were covered.

Disappointed as we were, we had no choice but to remain under that stage with our hunger. Many people made speeches as we prayed for them to finish and to begin the parade that would lead everyone through town and away from us, which, in time, happened.

Tired and hungry at the end of our worthless quest, we left the stage in the same way we entered it.

Due to the fact that we were so hungry and no one seemed to be around, we walked about the waterfront area and picked up bits and pieces of chicken and anything else we found to eat that had been left on the ground. For drinks we drained old soda cans, and thus ended our worthless quest to see if we could view the Queen's panty.

Now today as a man I wonder. If they had caught us then, what would have become of us? What type of charge would they have placed upon us? In any case we did what we did when we did it. Personally, I for one would like to apologize to the Queen. I was just a crazy little boy.

© 2000 Curtney Chinnery

Photo by Gerald Singer

Curtney Chinnery

BOOK PEOPLE

By Curtney Chinnery

When it comes to tourists, I as a child saw very few. Reason being is because in those days, which were the 50s and 60s, not many yachtsmen would venture across to Jost Van Dyke.

I for one used to call white folk "Book People," for that's the only place I used to see them, in books or magazines.

I remember one day in Great Harbour, Jost Van Dyke, near where Foxy's is today. It was the first time I came in physical contact with a white person.

It happened one day while a white boy and girl were playing ball. I was asked to join in. This for me was a great privilege, and, happy as can be I played with them.

From the paleness of their skin, and due to the fact that I

could see the blue veins beneath their skin, the thought was placed in my mind that they were soft and fragile. This in turn created a sense of fear about touching or grabbing them too hard. When the fellow's sister hit the beach ball in the air, both him and I chased after it. He tripped and fell, causing me to fall directly on top of him.

In any case, seeing he wasn't harmed I asked him with a little shyness, "Can I touch your hand?"

He looked me in the eye and got serious. Then he answered without a smile, "Sure, but only if I can touch you next."

With my pointing finger I reached out at his arm. At first softly I poked his skin. He did the same, but to my chest.

It seemed to me that he might have had thoughts of me being fragile, the same way I thought of him. Something like me thinking he was soft as a jellyfish and his thoughts that I may be soft as chocolate pudding.

It was my first touching or being in the company of someone white. A twist of fate made it to be the same for that boy. It was exactly the same.

The kid and I became friends that moment. When the yacht left Great Harbour, I watched with the hope that they would return someday. For almost two months, I would make my way to the bay in order to check if their vessel had returned.

That was my first dealing with the so-called white man.

HOOKADOE

By Curtney Chinnery

Now let's venture into childhood games of trickery we played with or on each other. This particular game of a trick was played on three people, a fellow who used to be called Blackbird, my brother by mother, Abraham, and myself. This game was played by the fellow we used to call Hookadoe. Hookadoe had a minor birth defect. The middle of his left foot from his big toe back to his ankle or heel was curved. Therefore he walked with something of a lick-wobble. At times we would call him lick-foot, in teasing him. At times we would say things concerning his defect, such as, "Hey Hookadoe, I hear that when your mother was giving birth to you, you couldn't wait to come out. You tried to run out of her and your left foot got caught up inside. And that's how your foot got bent up and twisted."

Our partner, Hookadoe, was a fellow who could handle

verbal abuse very well. Needless to say, one day our friend Hookadoe decided to get even by playing what I call a very unfair embarrassing technical game on Abraham, Blackbird and myself.

It all started one day at the Roadtown, Tortola waterfront, which was to us a place of play and a place where we generate funds by various means, such as diving for coins thrown to us by visiting tourists.

In any case being children, at times we dove and swam without clothes. Sometimes we would play what we call the "pillie-pulling game." Meaning, while swimming we'll try and catch each other off guard, and grab and pull one another's private parts.

One day we got out of the water where we were engaging in a game of pillie-pulling. When we sat at the side of the Customs Building, my brother Abraham turned to Hookadoe and asked him this: "Hey Hookadoe, how come your pillie is bigger than ours?"

Bear in mind that we at the time were nine, ten and eleven years old. We lacked knowledge of Hookadoe's true age. His age at the time was about 18 going on 19. Being he looked young he led us to believe his true age was 13 years old. Blackbird and I got curious concerning my brother's question to Hookadoe. We also wanted to know how it was possible for his pillie to be so much larger than ours.

Our friend Hookadoe realized that moment was the moment to get even with us. Hookadoe said, "I grew it to this size by using the egg of a thrushie bird." He went on to explain and to give us a bit of instruction on how to enlarge our pillies. We listened carefully to his instructions.

Hookadoe went on to say, "First you have to go into the hills and locate the nest of a thrushie bird. It must be a nest from the highest of the mountain. The nest, however, must be with eggs." He explained that the process must be done while in the tree.

In our minds we thought our friend Hookadoe had found a way to cheat in the aspect of growth concerning manhood, feeling if we did that and enlarged our private parts, we too would become lucky in becoming a man by cheating the laws of nature. So we decided to engage.

We were told that this process must be performed over a period of three days. The process was this: Once locating a nest with eggs, we must take a bird egg apiece while in the tree. We were to take an egg, crack it, and rub the interior substance on our pillies, and let the wind dry it, then leave. Keep in mind we did the process for three days. The other part of the instruction was that we were not to wash, meaning for three days we did not swim at the waterfront, nor took a bath.

In our minds we truly thought our pillies were changing size after the second day. As being an adult today I realize why our minds gave us the idea of growth. Our penises to us felt heavier. The reason for that was only because of the built-up sticky substance of the bird egg that dried and made us feel as if it was growing.

The third day fell on the weekend. Therefore, we all met

at the waterfront. When Hookadoe arrived, We told him
that we followed his instructions concerning pillie growth.
The fellow just fell to the ground and started to laugh saying,
"You stupid fools, it was only a joke!"

Today I have no choice but to say to Hookadoe, "Good show
buddy! You finally got even. And may you rest in peace." This
young fellow was the best swimmer of all of us, yet I was told
that he drowned while diving. If I am correct I think that
was the last pillie game we played after finding out that
Hookadoe was 18 going on 19 years of age.

A NOSE FOR DOGS

By Jack Andrews

I was living in Cathrineberg, high on the mountain overlooking Great Cinnamon Bay and the British Virgin Islands beyond. From there I could look right down on the beautiful white sand beach at Peter Bay, where I was building my new dream home in paradise.

At the time, I had a little black poodle named Pepe, who I took everywhere with me. People were so accustomed to seeing us together that I was known on the island as "the guy with the little black dog."

As construction of the beach house progressed, it became more and more difficult to bring Pepe with me. There were loaders, concrete trucks and all kinds of heavy equipment coming and going all day. As much as it broke my heart, I began leaving him alone at the house, while I was down at the construction site. As I'd prepare to leave each morning, I'd pick Pepe up and tell him he had to stay home by himself; and he always knew what I meant. You could see it in those little black eyes, that sad look of dejection. When I'd put him down, he would scurry over to his pillow and pout. As I left, he would start to howl with the saddest, most pathetic sounding cry.

At noon, I'd head back up the hill to say hello and keep him company during lunch.

One day I arrived home at lunchtime and called out, "I'm home, Pepe." But there was no answer, no happy little, "bark, bark, you came home to me." No piddle next to the door when I walked in, and, NO PEPE!

The screen door was ajar. Pepe was gone.

At first I thought he must have gone to try to find me at the beach house. To get there, he would have to make his way down the steep gravel road that switched back six times before meeting the North Shore Road, then go a half mile along that road to the driveway that led down to the beach. Nonetheless, he had already done this once before.

I drove back to the job site, but Pepe was nowhere to be seen. Next I went to my superintendent's house. His wife was home nursing her new baby. I called in to her, "Have you seen Pepe around? I can't find him."

"No", she said, "but there was something going on out in the bush this morning." She explained that every once in a while, the island donkeys come up through the woods and her three warrior chows go out after them. That morning, the chows had taken off in pursuit of what she thought were donkeys. She wasn't sure what had happened but there was "a heck of a racket for quite some time."

I was sick with panic! I started searching the bush, hollering at the top of my lungs and whistling for Pepe. I expected to find his furry carcass any moment, but nothing. No blood, no fur, no Pepe.

I went to the police station to report him missing, then to the taxi stand to pass the word among the taxi drivers who have their own island communication system, and then I went back to the job. There was still no sign of him. I felt a sick feeling deep in the pit of my stomach.

Back to the house, calling, whistling, all along the road. Maybe he had taken a wrong turn, and had gone down one of the other two driveways off the shore road – Mrs. Hall's or the park ranger's.

I drove down each driveway, calling out, not a sign anywhere. Next I drove to the other two beaches, Trunk and Cinnamon, picturing him headed for food or people. Asking around, park rangers, beachgoers, concessionaires, taxi drivers; no one had seen him.

As I drove from Trunk Bay to the top of the switchback at the main entrance to Peter Bay, two local men were installing a new donkey-guard across the road. One of the men was John Gibney.

John was born and brought up on St. John. He is a man of the earth, six foot six, lanky and muscular with shoulder-length blond hair, handsome chiseled features, and intense brown eyes that glint when he speaks to you with with his slight West Indian accent.

As I pulled up to where he was working, John asked, "Papa Jack, where is Pepe?" He had immediately noticed I wasn't carrying him on my arm or in my lap with his head out the window.

I said, "John, he's lost, have you seen him?"

"No, I haven't," he replied. John put down his shovel and said, "I'll go find him."

I told John that I had already looked everywhere around here. John pulled his shoulders back stiffly and held his head up with his nose in the air. Breathing in through his nose, he said, "Papa Jack, I got a nose for animals. I can find him. I'll be right back." John abruptly turned away, lifting his nose in the air as if to smell the scent, then started down the road with his head tilted back, sniffing from side to side.

By then, it was late afternoon and I decided to check back at the jobsite and pass the word to all the workers to keep an eye out when they headed home. I then drove back up the hill and decided to take another look down the park ranger's driveway in the hope of finding him at home to ask about Pepe.

When I pulled up near the front door, the ranger came out of the house to see what I wanted and I told him about Pepe. He said he had been at the house since nine in the morning and if Pep had come around, his "bush cats" would have chased him away, but there had been no noise or strange activity all day. These "bush cats" get to be about twenty-five pounds and are ferocious fighters. Two of them would tear little eight-pound Pepe to shreds.

Just then, John walked down the driveway and saw us standing there and said, "He's around here somewhere, I can smell him."

The ranger assured John that he must be wrong, because his cats hadn't moved and if the dog were anywhere around, they would have made mincemeat out of him.

All of a sudden, John jerked his head up as if he had been hit under the chin. He abruptly turned his head to the right and pointed his nose toward the hillside behind the house and exclaimed, "He's right up there in the bush, I'll go get him!" and he immediately crouched down and started making his way through the dense underbrush.

"I found him, Papa Jack! I found him! He's right over here!"

I headed for John's voice, and there was Pepe. He was at the bottom of a 15-foot stone cliff, hopelessly entangled in the barbed thorns of a bush known as catch-and-keep. He had been trapped there all day in the ninety-degree heat and was dehydrated and near death from exhaustion.

John reached into the thorny bushes and tried to free Pepe, who was in such a state of panic that he started biting at John's already scratched-up and bloodied hands.

I scaled down the side of the cliff, and poor Pepe was totally ensnared in the catch-and-keep. As he would try to move, the thorns would just tear into his flesh. Pepe was yelping and crying out with pain. It was awful, but with John's help, I was able to get Pep untangled and into my arms. At that point I choked up with emotion and began to cry.

I am certain that if it hadn't been for John Gibney and his nose for dogs, I never would have seen my faithful little companion again.

© 2000 Jack Andrews

PAPA DOC

By John Gibney

From whence he came, I have no idea; whither he fled, not a clue.

He was a cross between Popeye the Sailor Man and a main-drag Vegas loan shark, a paternal hank of angelic white hair ringing his nearly bald pate. His beady thrushie eyes could soften and radiate kindness to a schoolboy with a quarter in his hand. Yet in a brief instant those same eyes could be as cold as a viper ready to strike, if the kid tried to sneak an extra dollop of catsup on his half-cooked greasy french-fries.

Yes, we were afraid of Papa Doc; yet I, for one, held him in awe.

One day, the yard across from where the Chase Bank now stands was the home of Henry "Limejuice" Richards and his family, and then, presto, the next day, a plywood and putty stand materialized.

Red and white stripes, multicolored strings of plastic flags, multiple roofs, deep fryers, drink coolers, plastic chairs with greasy splay-footed plastic tables to match, and, glory of glories, a state-of-the-art 1966 instant ice cream machine with levers and dials, bells and whistles.

From a narrow slot in the plywood, we witnessed Papa Doc pouring in packets of "Easy-Freeze" ice cream powder, a garden hose connection amidships where water did its magic. An old Texaco oil drum on the roof easily took the place of a municipal water supply, and the reliable force of gravity took the place of the electric water pump.

At the business end of this space-age, stainless steel, ice cream cow, were not two but three taps. Man had yet to land on the moon, but we were launched into the ice cream age, three flavors: chocolate, vanilla and strawberry.

Papa Doc must also be given the credit for bringing the Styrofoam cup to St. John, also recycling. After the morning coffee rush had cleared, we would see Papa Doc collecting all the used cups, crushing them in his wizened Midas hands into an empty gallon can of Miss Filbert's Margarine. Then the little white chips were dumped unceremoniously into a Waring Blender, a cup of Mazola Oil and, voila, there is white paste poured into the Easy-Freeze Machine. "Filler," muttered Papa Doc between his stained teeth, taking a pull on his Tampico Cigar and spitting out the bitten-off end.

Christmas was coming and the Christmas Winds were picking

up. One morning on the way to school, we met Papa Doc in his yard under the plum tree with some six brand-new shiny Honda 50 motorcycles in a neat row and six big cardboard boxes with "Honda Motors" written in English and the rest in Japanese.

Sweat on his brow and an adjustable wrench in his hands, "God-damned Japanese!" he spat, as he tried to read the instruction manual by turning it upside down.

A rearview mirror was placed in its handlebar anchor, and the first motorcycle was ready to be rented out. Bending his white, hairless, chicken legs, Papa Doc stooped down to his reflection, his left hand preening the 13 remaining hairs on his head until they stood up firmer and straighter than any fighting cock in his yard. On his face the splendor of a man who had just broken the bank at Caesar's Palace.

"Piece of cake!" said Papa Doc. Yes, he was a genius.

Throughout the day, we checked out his progress on the remaining "units." Not entertaining the purest of thoughts, we focused our attention on the connection where the main wire harness met the starting switch.

They were fast, dependable, and light enough so that they could be easily lifted over Papa Doc's chain link fence in the evening after he had gone home to bed, and just as easily replaced early in the morning before he got up.

The Hondas were great, the timing perfect. On cool December nights, the hills and valleys of St. John rang with the sounds of small-bore Japanese motors wound out to the max.

Their nemesis proved to be the hill leaving Lameshur Bay, soon to be the site of Project Tektite. Project Tektite was an underwater habitat where brave American aquanauts were to spend some 60 days under water.

The aquanauts' record-breaking 60 days under water couldn't hold a candle to Papa Doc's Hondas that have now spent 33-odd years under the waters of that same bay – and still counting.

The next mornng, we checked all the possibilities of stowing away to avoid the ire of Papa Doc.

Even on tropical St. John, where the seasonal change is not as dramatic as elsewhere in the world, there is a feeling of rebirth and renewal when winter turns to spring. Trees and bushes begin to flower, attracting the birds and the bees, and both man and beast experience an increased degree of friskiness.

That spring, Papa Doc expanded his operation. A new plywood wing had been erected at the back. It was whispered amongst us that he had imported some women from Puerto Rico. Late in April, I slipped out of school to go by Oscar's Diner for a mid-morning soda.

Oscar had taken over the former "Baptist Beanery" at the back half of the former VI Aids Building. VI Aids was the only drugstore on St. John and stood in the location now occupied by the Scotiabank trailer. Papa Doc walked over and ordered a coffee from Oscar. When someone asked him why he crossed the street to drink Oscar's coffee rather than his own brew, he just winked at me. That Papa Doc was feeling his oats was evident, as evident as if Popeye the Sailor Man had fallen into a spinach truck.

"Rosa is pregnant," he gloated, his posture not betraying his age, which must have been in his late 70s. I believed he was referring to one of the pretty Latina women, and sure enough, she began to show. Papa Doc began to get positively cocky, strutting his stuff, while the quality of his food began to decline. The yard fowl, which were much more numerous then, had taken heavy losses at the hands of Papa Doc and his henchmen. The chicken legs from his deep fryer were tougher than boot leather. Papa Doc became a regular at Oscar's, while his Coney Island-style stand became more of a "tourist trap."

One morning in early November as the Christmas Winds again began to blow, we passed Papa Doc's on the way to school. The plywood shutters were nailed down. The plastic chairs inside. The happy rhythms of the Salsa music stilled. It was whispered about that Rosa gave birth, and although DNA testing was not available in those days, there could be little doubt in any seeing man's eyes that there was no way that the baby could be his. Papa Doc was crushed.

One day soon after, two big trucks came from St. Thomas and gutted Popa Doc's stand right down to the plastic chairs.

Then two G-men from Chicago showed up flashing badges and mug shots.

It seems that Papa Doc was a notorious con man. His Havana stories made more sense now. He had, it seems, arrived with a line of credit, opened the business on credit, then when he smelled the hounds, sold everything to the highest bidder for hard, cold cash and moved on to greener pastures.

Maybe some in the long line of carpetbaggers, unscrupulous realtors and con men who have followed in his footsteps have stopped to wonder why their actions have barely raised an eyebrow among St. Johnians.

Why, because we knew Papa Doc.

THE BLUE HERON

By John Gibney

August is a heavy sultry month in these hurricane islands. The wind will die and the sun transforms the sea into angry clouds. The tradewinds fall back all the way to the Cape Verde Islands off the African continent. There is a heaviness, a foreboding that one can feel in their bones, the brooding of a tropical hurricane.

My mother told me, "John, the old-timers say that when the little leaflets on the coconut fronds don't move at all, it is 'hurricane weather.'"

In later years, I have read that one Atlantic hurricane can generate and release more energy than all the atomic bombs ever exploded in wartime and in tests combined.

August also sees the flamboyant trees fading their passionate colors, and the lush hillsides changing from overpowering greenness to more pastel tones.

It was in August of 1959 that Dr. J. Robert Oppenheimer, the so-called "father of the atomic bomb," came to stay with my family here at Hawksnest. I had just turned five years old and had no idea of who this person was. But as I watched this extraordinary man, there was an ethereal, vaporous quality that haunted me at the time and continues to haunt me up until this day.

The doctor would walk the beach from end to end and back again, always at the point where the sea and the sand meet. His footprints were quickly erased by the slight ripples of the glass-smooth sea.

There is a blue heron bird that lives in the seagrape trees here at the beach behind our house. It was born in the mangrove trees in the swamp some two years ago. It is grown now, and every evening it walks the beach as the bright vivid colors of our tropical day give way to the gentle pastels of the evening. Because of the long, stick-like bird legs, the frail avian body, the stooped, labored posture with skinny elbows protruding out from behind, and the measured bird gait, we have taken to calling him "Dr. Oppenheimer."

As a boy of five I knew nothing of the bomb. The power, the glory, the fear, the guilt. I was a lonely little boy – wild – we had no neighbors. There was only my brother and sister. We had no TV in the house nor was there one on the entire island. I did have an imaginary friend I called Mr. No-Name. Instead of TV we would watch the cloud formations in the west as the sun was going down. All the way from Trinidad to Cuba, the

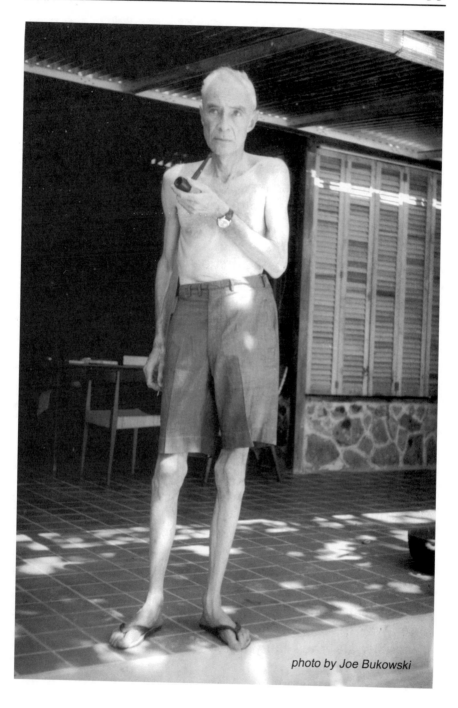

photo by Joe Bukowski

cloud-line follows the islands, as any sailor knows. We saw it all – elephants, lions, horses, camels, armies marching off to war, pirate ships and magnificent cities. How true that which Uncle Albert said: "Imagination is much more powerful than knowledge."

I was born in St. John in 1954. My parents were both writers. My mother wrote romance short stories for ladies' magazines, *Vogue, Red Book, McCall's, Ladies Home Journal*. My father was an artist, painter, sculptor and mechanical genius as well as a writer.

My parents were among the first beatniks. They lived in communes in the late 30s and early 40s with such travelers as Thomas Merton, the monk; Robert Lax, the poet; Ad Reinhart, the father of pop art; and Herman Wouk, who penned the classic *Don't Stop the Carnival*.

They first came to St. John In 1946. Father left his job as editor for *New Republic*, my mother hers as editor at *Vogue*. They bought Hawksnest Beach in 1949 and built a house there. In those days there was no Northshore Road and all the building materials had to be brought in by sloop.

Dr. Oppenheimer had been one of the targets of the Senator McCarthy red witch-hunt. There were allegations of shared information, family alliances, espionage, etc.

How he came to our troubled family, I'm not sure, but St. John has always been a haven for escapees and refugees of all kinds. I believe the doctor and his wife felt that they could hide away from the world, shielded by the remoteness, the tranquility and the beauty of the island.

How powerless we are to change even what has just happened in the last split second.

Shiva, the Hindu Shatterer of Worlds. The power of the Destroyer was so glorified on that morning in 1945 when the desert rains cleared and the great minds saw a "light as of a thousand suns." But by eventide, the thousand suns had faded to shades of pastel. In the water, that original mirror, in the stillness of the Creator all things become clear.

I have always understood Lord Aston's famous quote, "Power corrupts, but absolute power corrupts, absolutely," to be referring to the ill-gotten power of tyrants or perhaps the power of riches or prestige. But the love of the power of one's own beloved creation, especially one so powerful as the bomb, seems to bring another kind of corruption.

It is strange, but the Hopi Indians of New Mexico, who inhabit that desert where the bomb was born and the scientists drew their inspiration, have in their religion the story of "Coyote the Trickster" who sneaks up on God's mountain and steals the fire of the Almighty.

What an enigma Oppenheimer was. One of *Life Magazine*'s 100 Men of the Century, revered by his students, so powerful yet so powerless, so frail, so conscious, yet so yearning for oblivion.

I have heard that on the night following the Hiroshima bomb, there was a Champagne party to toast the successful blast and the destruction of their target, and only Oppenheimer, his wife, Kitty, and General Leslie Groves, the military attaché, attempted to raise their glasses as the men, women and children of Hiroshima dragged their charred skins behind them or sought direction through their burned-out eyes.

In that moment when time itself was split, Pandora's box was so savagely pried open, and the atomic scientists themselves knew sin. I have read that Albert Einstein said before his death, "I have become as a child before the universe, I know nothing," or words to that effect. Perhaps Uncle Albert sailed lightly into paradise. I just wish that I could play with Mr. No-Name again.

I believe that Dr. Oppenheimer walked a plateau between worlds, with the accuser on one hand and the savior or the deep blue sea on the other. No amount of Stolichnaya vodka or Turkish heroin could ever give proper salve to a soul thus tormented.

In 1962, during the Cuban Missile Crisis, the Oppenheimers were on island and had come to my parents' house for martinis. At some point toward dusk, a large array of dark clouds had formed down to the west over St. Thomas. I will never forget the expression on all of the grownups' faces when a large mushroom-shaped cloud formed out toward the northwest over the cays in the general direction of Havana or Miami: "Oh my God! What have we done...." I slunk out the back to go talk to Mr. No-Name.

In one moment in the heat of the battle, the great mental and physical forces giving their all to develop this bomb – in one microsecond – I see the blue heron bird walking Hawksnest Beach, the day fades to night and the force of life itself ebbs in the tide. The ocean blends into gentle pastel shades and merges with the fading evening sky.   © 2000 John Gibney

THE MAN WHO HAD A CRAB IN HIS EAR

By Gerald Singer

The following account was told to me by Dr. Robert Walker, who practiced medicine on St. John in the 1980s.

One afternoon, a man was taking a swim at Trunk Bay when, all of a sudden, he felt something go inside his ear. He swam to shore, stood on the sandy beach and tried to get it out.

He used all the everyday remedies that people use for this sort of problem. He tapped on the opposite side of his head with his hand. He jumped up and down while tilting his head to one side. He put his finger in his ear and wiggled it. Nothing worked.

The man was experiencing a great deal of discomfort. He could hear a kind of buzzing or scratching, and he had the distinct feeling that something alive was moving about in his ear. He felt dizzy and nauseous. The man decided to seek medical attention and drove to the clinic.

The sensation he was feeling became more and more disturbing, and by the time he was finally able to see the doctor, he was beside himself with anxiety and worry. Dr. Walker, the attending physician, thought he might have to sedate his nervous patient. He decided not to, and began his examination, which quickly revealed the source of the problem: a small crab was inside the man's ear.

(Those of you who enjoy swimming at our beautiful beaches; please understand that crabs don't usually go in people's ears. It is, in fact, the only time that anyone has ever heard of such a thing.)

The knowledge of what was causing the problem did not alleviate the man's anxiety; it actually increased it. He began to plead with the doctor: "Please, please, hurry, Doc, please GET THE CRAB OUT OF MY EAR!"

The doctor got to work. Armed with magnifying glasses, a special light and medical tweezers, he set about the task of extracting the crab. The patient squirmed, and the doctor exhorted him to sit still, and, after what seemed an eternity to all concerned, the doctor successfully removed the crustacean intruder.

"I've got it!" said Dr. Walker.

"Thank God!" exclaimed his grateful patient.

"And here's the culprit," said the proud doctor, as he placed the captured crab on his hand and brought it into view for the man to see.

At this point, something quite unexpected occurred. Just as soon as the crab was released from the grip of the tweezers, it jumped out of the doctor's hand, scurried up the patient's arm and leapt right back into the same ear!

NOTE:

After another fifteen minutes of crab hunting, and apologizing to an extremely upset patient, the good doctor was finally able to recapture the crab; this time, he did not give it a second opportunity to escape.

WILLIAM THORNTON

BY GERALD SINGER

Once upon a time, braves of the Algonquin nation met at the foot of a hill, not far from the banks of the mighty Potomac River, in order to hold their councils. Today, another nation holds its councils on this very spot. Their leaders erected an extraordinary building on the top of that hill, which has become a symbol of the most powerful nation on earth.

The building on the top of that hill is the United States Capitol. This magnificent monument was designed by a man who was born on a remote island, educated as a doctor, lacked formal training as an architect, and may be best known (at least in the Virgin Islands) for lending his name to a popular floating bar and restaurant anchored in The Bight at Norman Island. His name was William Thornton and he was born in 1759 in Great Harbour on Jost Van Dyke.

The events leading up to this unlikely connection tell an amazing tale.

After the successful American Revolution in 1776, the first congresses of the new nation were inconveniently convened in eight different cities: Philadelphia, Baltimore, Lancaster, York, Princeton, Annapolis, Trenton, and New York City.

In 1787, the U.S. Constitution provided for a permanent capital to be established, a federal district unto itself, part of no state, where the functions of the emerging government would be centralized in one location. The new capital, the District of Columbia, was to be named Washington, D.C., in honor of the country's first president.

Formal procedures were established and qualified men were appointed to make the many decisions that this far-reaching project would require. In actuality, the inevitable atmosphere of chaos allowed hidden dramas, under-the-table deals, secret personal connections and international political alliances to determine who would be in charge of what.

George Washington wanted to appoint the idiosyncratic French engineer, Pierre Charles L'Enfant, as the chief city planner. L'Enfant was not well liked and had several powerful enemies, including John Jay, the first Chief Justice of the Supreme Court. It was only under intense pressure from President Washington himself that a reluctant Congress approved L'Enfant's appointment.

L'Enfant's vision of the capital city was inspired by the graceful and classic beauty epitomized by the Palace and Gardens at Versailles in his native Paris. The streets and avenues would be laid out on a geometric grid, which would be overlaid by diagonals.

The hill chosen as the site for the District's predominant building, the Capitol, was described by L'Enfant as "a pedestal waiting for a monument."

The most enormous of L'Enfant's many tasks was to plan, design and supervise the construction of the U.S. Capitol building. The French engineer, however, proved to be extremely difficult to work with. He refused to recognize the authority of the commissioners, who were ultimately responsible for the project and who were, in effect, his bosses.

In addition, he continued to irritate other influential people. For example, parallel avenues running north-south were to be named after states; east-west streets were to be named after letters of the alphabet – that is, A Street, B Street, C Street, etc. The systematic progression of lettered streets was interrupted, however, with the omission of J Street. The childish L'Enfant did not want his enemy, John Jay, to be so honored.

When L'Enfant personally and without authorization tore up the porch of a rich landowner because it obstructed the path of the proposed New Jersey Avenue, the commissioners called the Frenchman in for a showdown. In that meeting, L'Enfant was asked to produce the design for the Capitol building. The engineer's response was that it was unnecessary to have a written plan, because he carried the design "in his head."

That was it for L'Enfant. He was fired. His city-planning duties were taken over by his assistant, Andrew Ellicot, who was more sympathetic to the compromises that were, from time to time, demanded by established private landholdings.

George Washington and the commissioners, however, now needed to find a new architect to produce a plan and construct a Capitol building worthy of their great vision.

In order to find a suitable candidate for the job, Secretary of State Thomas Jefferson arranged for a competition in which a prize of $500 and a city lot would be awarded to the architect who produced the best plan by the middle of July.

An advertisement was placed in newspapers throughout the new nation. The contest was well underway by the time word of it reached an interested party on the faraway island of Tortola in the Virgin Islands: Dr. William Thornton.

Thornton, who was born in 1759 in Great Harbour, Jost Van Dyke, received his early education in England and later studied medicine at the University of Edinburgh. At the time of the contest, he was a practicing physician on Tortola. The young doctor was also a brilliant amateur architect, having previously won a competition for the design of a new building for the Philadelphia Library.

Thornton was intrigued with the idea of designing the Capitol and immediately wrote a letter asking permission to enter the contest, even though he knew his entry would arrive late.

By the time Thornton's drawings reached the temporary Capitol in Philadelphia, the contest was indeed closed. Undaunted, he made an appointment to see George Washington, determined to show him the work.

It turned out that Washington was not satisfied with any of the designs that had been presented in the competition, and when he saw Thornton's plans, he was extremely pleased. Washington then sent Thornton to submit his plans to the commissioners who were in charge of the project, along with a letter urging them to reconsider the contest deadline.

THE UNITED STATES CAPITOL

Today, the Capitol covers a ground area of 175,170 square feet, or about 4 acres, and has a floor area of approximately 16½ acres. Its length, from north to south, is 751 feet 4 inches; its greatest width, including approaches, is 350 feet. Its height above the base line on the east front to the top of the Statue of Freedom is 288 feet; from the basement floor to the top of the dome is an ascent of 365 steps. The building contains approximately 540 rooms and has 658 windows (108 in the dome alone) and approximately 850 doorways."

(Office of the Curator)

In the letter, Washington also praised Thornton's work, writing, "Grandeur, Simplicity and Convenience appear to be well combined in the plan of Dr. William Thornton." Thomas Jefferson, who was also a notable architect, characterized the design as "simple, noble, beautiful and excellently arranged."

According to Thornton's plan, the building would be comprised of three segments. The central portion, covered by a dome, would be flanked by two symmetrical rectangular wings, which would house the Senate and House of Representatives.

The commissioners agreed with Washington and Jefferson. They pronounced the young doctor from Jost Van Dyke to be the winner of the contest, and the Capitol was erected, substantially along the lines of his blueprints.

When the actual construction began, Thornton moved to the emerging District of Columbia. He became a friend of George Washington and was appointed one of the three commissioners who were responsible for building the city. Later, Thornton was selected as the first Commissioner of Patents, a post he occupied until his death in 1828.

THE SUCKER

BY GERALD SINGER

On St. John, everyone seems to know one another – if not directly, at least peripherally. This is a mixed blessing. It offers a network of community support and a warm feeling of belonging, but you give up anonymity and a certain degree of privacy. So if you screw up, everyone knows about it.

One day, two individuals, both well known on St. John, wanted to smoke an herb that, although not particularly dangerous or addictive, is illegal. For this reason, the two island residents decided to conduct the forbidden activity where they wouldn't readily be seen.

As the two friends happened to be in Cruz Bay at the time, they walked up one of the National Park trails that begins in the vicinity of town. About five minutes up the trail, they came upon what appeared to be an ideal location. A large flat rock in the shade of a mampo tree lay partly hidden just off the main trail and would provide a comfortable and private place to sit down and have an illegal smoke.

The first man sat down and immediately jumped up. The rock was already occupied by a small cactus commonly called a sucker. The barbed spines went through his pants and became lodged in his buttocks. The man cried out in pain and surprise and followed it up with a colorful string of profanities.

Sucker spines are difficult to remove once they pierce the skin. This is due to the barbed point and the segmented construction of the spine, which causes it to break off when a person tries to pull it out. A chemical irritant on the spine causes puncture wounds to be painful, and if the spine is allowed to remain imbedded in the skin, it can be annoying at least and cause an infection at worst. The spines usually work themselves out, but the best thing is to remove them, which is just what the man tried to do.

This job was obviously difficult. He couldn't see what he was doing, nor could he get a good grip on pulling the things out.

He needed help and this task fell to his friend.

He pulled down his pants and leaned against the trunk of the tree. His buddy then put on his glasses, and with the intense concentration of a surgeon, struggled to remove the imbedded spines.

The two men were suddenly aware of another presence. They looked up to see a thoroughly shocked National Park Ranger standing on the trail staring at them. To make matters worse, it was one of the rangers whom they recognized as having been around St. John for a long time.

The man with the sucker spines in his behind got the picture right away. A locally famous ladies' man, his immediate thought was that this story would not tell well around St. John. But although he was usually cool-headed and a smooth talker, he could not pull up his pants quickly enough and he began to stumble over his words.

With his pants halfway pulled up, he shouted to the ranger, "Officer, I know what you're thinking, but I can explain – it's not what it looks like! You see, I sat on a cactus and...."

He didn't get a chance to finish. The ranger backed up and mumbled something to himself.

"Officer, I can explain, please listen!" But it was to no avail. The ranger didn't say another word. He just hurriedly continued down the trail, never looking back.

The two men returned to town, relieved, at least, that their illegal herbology had not been discovered, but worried about the explanation they would have to make to their friends if the ranger told this tale around town, and whether or not they would be believed.

John Gibney and Hermon Smith - January 2001
Photo by Gerald Singer

A BULL STORY

BY GERALD SINGER

Back in the early 1980s, Mr. Aegis Marsh, the venerable St. Johnian, now deceased, approached three strapping young island men, each a character in his own right, and asked them to help him do a job. The men, well-known on the island today, were John Gibney, Hermon Smith and Buster Brady.

It seems that Mr. Aegis had six bulls that were loose in the bush. Never having been shown a plot plan, the animals would, from time to time, cross into the territory of the newly created Virgin Islands National Park. Something needed to be done because, Mr. Aegis explained, "the National Park is giving me hell." The solution, according to Mr. Aegis, was to round up the bulls and bring them to the beach at Maho Bay. There they would be loaded on a barge and transported to St. Thomas to be sold.

And that is how, bright and early the next morning, Gibney, Smith and Brady presented themselves to Mr. Aegis, ready for a day's work.

The bulls were somewhere in the thick bush in the lower flats of the Maho Bay Valley. The four men, armed with ropes, sticks and machetes, made their way to the area around the gut (rocky stream bed) on which the errant bulls were wandering about.

The first animal they found was about a football field away from where they had to take him. Unfortunately it was not a football field that they had available to them. It was a swampy marsh, thickly tangled with thorny plants and with patches of slippery mud and pools of slimy swamp water as much as five feet deep.

Mr. Aegis himself placed the first rope around the bull, using a long stick fashioned with a noose that he deftly slid around its stout neck. From then on, the job was in the hands of the three younger men. They began by tying the free end of the rope to a tree in order to prevent the beast from running off. Next, they tied two additional ropes around the bull's neck so that each man could control one line.

The bull was uncooperative. He knocked his captors into the thorny plants and sent them sliding into the gooey marsh. He had to be coaxed, dragged, prodded and tricked every inch of the way. At one time, the furious and powerful bull tore the rope from the men's hands and tried to charge them, head lowered, horns ready.

When that happened, one of the line handlers grabbed the

loose rope and wound it around a tree while the others scrambled to get out of the angry bull's way. Throughout the day, Mr. Aegis was careful to maintain his own safe distance from the proceedings.

It took over two hours to haul the obstinate animal out of the bush and onto the beach. When that arduous task was finally accomplished, the bloody, slime-covered, scraped-up bull-chasers still had five more bulls to contend with.

We will spare the gentle reader the details of these five further encounters, but although their bull-capturing technique improved somewhat, their physical and mental condition deteriorated progressively.

When, nearing sunset, the last bull was tied up on the beach at Big Maho, Mr. Aegis turned to his exhausted workers and asked, "Well, boys, how much do I owe you?"

It was John Gibney who replied, "Whatever you think it was worth, Mr. Aegis." The old man pulled out his billfold and handed each a twenty-dollar bill. Then, as the thoroughly demoralized men began their long walk back home, Mr. Aegis called out after them, "Do you suppose you boys could get here a little earlier tomorrow? The barge from St. Thomas will be here at daybreak."

The next day only Gibney showed up, and by his account, it was even worse than the previous day, but that's another story.

"Didn't I make you feel like you were the only man..."

as sung by Janis Joplin, **Piece of My Heart**

ART AND JANIS

BY BOB TIS

I come for the stories. And, of course, for the companionship. Cartoon large blue eyes roll in acceptance, as Art fingers a slice of a mango I just picked from his jungle yard and sliced up with my Swiss Army knife. We are out in the bush. A steep dirt road winds downhill to a locked gate. Unlocked, the gate reveals a footpath through a jungle crowded with trash-picked treasures. The path leads to a living museum for the last remaining hippie.

Art's museum is a home built partly in cooperation with Mother Nature, Robinson-Crusoe style, employing two large turpentine trees. It is constructed from thick beams salvaged from the wreckage of 30 years of hurricanes and boatloads of memories. The walls are strewn with block and tackle from long-sunk schooners and smuggling ships. Bad art and hurricane lamps are everywhere; giant candles, Mardi Gras

Art "Art the Painter" Albricht

Photo by Gerald Singer

beads, a collection of colorful shirts and the assorted claptrap of 30 years on St. John decorate this un-electrified museum.

The mango sliced, I set my sights on a bucket of congealed floor wax, which I cut loose and feed to a homemade tiki torch. In the gloaming, the first Cuban tree frogs start to croak and Art eggs them on.

"Rrrbiit, rrribbbit." St. John's first hippie is clearly amused with the idea of talking to the frogs and his eyes grow even wider, reflecting their seasoned madness in the candlelight. The frogs, mistakenly imported from Castro's Cuba by some researchers in the 1970s, take up Art's gauntlet. We are met with a thunderous cacophony of croaks in the Caribbean night.

I go for the transistor radio to tune out the frogs. I pop another warmish Heineken and get Art a non-alcoholic Budweiser. No electricity means no fridge and ice melts too quickly for it to be economical. There could be thousands of dollars buried on the property from various Caribbean adventures but Art makes do on beans and rice and maybe an O'Douls if I bring some up to his museum.

I like to get out of Cruz Bay, where the noisy beach bars have a way of filling up with sunburned tourists in the winter. Tonight I'll camp out at the museum. Art and I will watch the still, moonless sky for satellites and rehash the business of the day.

The battery-powered rock 'n' roll radio brings us a nugget from the sixties and I coax Art into one of his favorite stories of how he met Janis Joplin in St. Thomas well over thirty years ago. It is a story I love. I am continually astounded by the attention to detail in my friend's storytelling. In Art's stories, the details never change, and I have learned first-hand that nothing varies from the original event.

"I missed the last bus," Art explains, talking about a night over thirty years ago like it was last week. "I was drinking in the waterfront bars and my boat was on the other side of the island in Red Hook.

"In those days, there were no cars going in that direction in the middle of the night and bars stayed open all night. It was about three in the morning, so I had a few hours to kill before I could hitch a ride home."

Art's hands begin to move and his eyes widen as he launches into this memoir. I easily picture him thirty years ago sitting on a barstool in an empty Charlotte Amalie watering hole, sipping on a draft beer and waiting for the sun.

"She walked in and went right for the jukebox. It was only the bartender and I and maybe some other rummy in the whole place. She didn't play her song, she played something else.

"She sat down next to me and ordered a shot of Southern Comfort. I was speechless. This was 1968 and Janis Joplin was a very big deal. I was trying hard to be cool and not to spook her.

"'You look familiar,' I told her.

"'Oh yeah, well just who do you think I look like?' Janis asked.

"'Frank Zappa' I told her.

"Janis loved it. She slapped me on the back and bought me a whiskey. Before I knew it she was gone, pushing her way out through the swinging doors just as fast as she came in. All of a sudden her music was playing on the jukebox.

"Word spread like wildfire that Janis was on St. Thomas. Two days later this guy I knew was telling me all about it. I didn't let on that I had already seen her. He said Janis wanted to go for a sailboat ride, but she didn't want to go with just anyone. She wanted to go with someone who was cool. I told the guy I would take Janis out the next day.

"At the time I had a nice wooden double-ender, about 30 feet long, with beautiful lines. The boat didn't have an engine but I didn't really need one. It was a nice sailing boat.

"There was a guy named Todd living on the boat with me. He was a real freak with hair down to his waist. He was a real ladies' man, too. I remember telling him we were going to take Janis out sailing and I know he didn't believe me.

"The day came and it was a little overcast and kind of blustery. It wasn't the best day, but it was a good day for sailing. The morning went by and Janis never showed up. I kept telling Todd to watch the dock with the binoculars so he could row in and get Janis. He still thought I was kidding.

"She showed up around 3 p.m., with a whole entourage of record company hangers-on. I was yelling to Todd that she was at the dock. When he finally saw her through the glasses, his jaw dropped. It took Todd three trips to get Janis and all her groupies out to the boat. When Janis got on board, she recognized me immediately.

"'I should have known it would be you,' she told me.

"They brought all sorts of food, chips, dips, olives, booze, all sorts of stuff you couldn't get in the Virgin Islands at the time. We put up the sails and it was obvious that most of them had never been on a boat before.

"Janis was scared at first, but after I explained to her the physics of the boat, the fact that the keel was so heavy it wouldn't allow us to capsize, she felt better. She just didn't want to tip over.

"Everybody else though, except Todd and myself, were terrified. We were slogging through some good chop, really sailing. Janis started to get into it and I let her hold the wheel. She took off her shirt and showed everybody her giant nipples.

"The guys in the record company crew were still griping. Some of them were throwing up. I think they had eaten some Quaaludes.

"After sailing for about twenty minutes, I came about and explained that everybody who wanted to go ashore had one chance, one chance only. I was sailing for the beach and when I said, 'Jump,' they could get off or spend the rest of the afternoon on the boat.

When I got to the beach, most everybody jumped off. A few guys wanted to stay but Todd and I just started tossing them into the ocean. After we pried the grip of the last guy off the starboard stay, we chucked him in the water and turned out to sea. Me, Todd and Janis.

"We slipped into a real nice reach and really started having fun. Janis loved sailing. Todd got naked and told Janis that he had always wanted to have sex with her, and how about now?

"'No thanks,' Janis said. 'But if you want to have me after one of my shows, you can. After I've made love to the whole audience for two hours, then you can have me.'

Art's wild eyes radiate when he gets to that part, his smile betraying just how vividly he remembers the day's events.

Art goes on to explain how he got to be friends with Janis over the next few weeks. He retells the story of listening to the first recording of her new album on the hotel room bed at Bluebeard's Castle Hotel. He retells the story of having dinner with Janis and a friend at *Escargot*, which was, at the time, the best restaurant in the Caribbean.

Art finishes this rock star story by retelling Janis's very tempting invitation, which resulted from his missed bus ride.

"'Janis said, you're from New York, come to Woodstock with me this summer, you can be my guest, I'll fly you up there.'

"I told her I had read in the paper that Woodstock wasn't going to happen, that they couldn't find a place for the concert.

"Janis said, 'Baby, I'm going to Woodstock this summer and so are a lot other people, you can bet that it's going to happen.'

"I didn't want to go back to New York. I had just bought the boat, so I stayed in the Virgin Islands," Art says ruefully.

So like time itself, Woodstock just sort of passed Art by in the Caribbean. In his museum, the cover from the very album that they listened to over three decades earlier is still tacked to a wall. In the photograph, you can see through Janis's oversized spectacles and look into her equally wide eyes. When you stare at the picture closely you can't help but think that Janis could have been Art's sister.

The album cover is faded and wilting, but her wide eyes are still clear behind the Hollywood glasses.

THE TOOTH

BY GERALD SINGER

While working as a boat captain for Delbert Parsons at Ocean Runner, I was given the assignment of taking a sweet and fun-loving family out on a boat charter to the British Virgin Islands. The family consisted of a mom and dad and their three children, a boy of 13 and two girls, 9 and 11.

We checked in at Jost Van Dyke and from there went to Norman Island to explore the famous Treasure Caves.

I stayed aboard the boat while the others snorkeled.

The family must have loved the experience because they were gone quite some time. When they returned, they told me that the older of the two girls had lost a tooth while she was snorkeling.

I asked the girl if I could see the tooth. Immediately the father spoke up and said that his daughter had probably just dropped the tooth into the water.

"Don't you believe in the tooth fairy?" I asked the girl. Again, the father answered for her, "not in this family." The girl then gave me a quick smile and showed us her missing tooth, which she had been hiding in her bathing suit.

In the course of the ensuing conversation, it came out that the tooth fairy was something of a family issue, and that the little girl had even written a story about it for school.

This is the little girl's story, as she related it to me.

"Once there were two ten-year-old girls who lived in the same town. One night both girls lost a baby tooth.

One of the girls had nice parents who believed in the tooth fairy. She put her tooth under her pillow that night and when she awoke, the tooth was gone, but there was a quarter in its place.

The other little girl had cheap, mean, stingy parents who didn't believe in the tooth fairy. They told the little girl to throw the worthless tooth in the garbage.

The next day both little girls went with the other school children on a trip to the zoo. The two of them stayed together, and walked away from the other children to see the gorilla. They didn't pay attention to the time, and the rest of the class left without them. They had to get home by themselves, but they weren't afraid because there was a bus that went right to where they lived.

The little girl who had the quarter from the tooth fairy, was able to get on the bus and go home, but the other little girl didn't have a quarter because her parents were mean and stingy and cheap so she couldn't take the bus. To make matters worse it began to rain – hard!

The little girl had to walk all the way home in the pouring rain, and she got pneumonia and died, and her cheap, stingy parents were to blame."

Our next stop on the snorkeling tour was the Indians, an area of coral reef where three giant rocks rise about 40 feet above the surface of the water.

This time, I put on my snorkeling gear and joined the family. Before we got in the water, the father asked the little girl what she was going to do with the tooth.

"Perhaps you should throw it overboard here," he suggested, "This is as beautiful a place as you'll be able to find anywhere in the world."

She said she intended to do just that, but first wanted to find the perfect place to leave her baby tooth.

We all jumped in the water and followed the little girl, who was holding the tooth tightly in her hand as she snorkeled around the rocks and over the reef.

The decision process lasted almost half an hour, and finally the little girl found the spot she was looking for. She let the tooth fall, and we all watched as it began its slow, gliding descent.

The tooth never reached its intended location. Within seconds after the little girl let it go, a yellowtail snapper, apparently thinking it to be a food item, snatched up the tooth and swam away with it.

THE SOLDIER AND THE PRIEST

By Gerald Singer

Gonzalo Guerrero was born in Palos, Spain in 1490. Historians believe that he was from a Jewish family that converted to Catholicism. We also know that he received at least some early education, as he was able to read and write.

Palos was the port of departure for Christopher Columbus's historic crossing of the Atlantic Ocean. On his safe return, rumors of gold and glory circulated among the young men of the city, and Palos was transformed almost overnight. An atmosphere of excitement and furor surrounded the bustling docks where ships were hastily being outfitted and provisioned, crewed by an international conglomeration of sailors and adventurers. When he became of age, Guerrero signed on with one of the many expeditions to the New World.

Jerónimo Aguilar was born in Ecija, Spain, about 1489. He

studied to be a Franciscan priest and traveled to the Americas for a different reason. He wanted to bring the Christian faith to the inhabitants of this remote part of the world.

So it came to be that both young men found themselves on the island of Hispaniola, the first Spanish stronghold in the New World. At that time, a conquistador by the name of Diego de Nicuesa was organizing an army to colonize the Caribbean coast of Central and South America. Both men joined: Guerrero as a foot soldier, Aguilar as a soldier of Christ.

Nicuesa had sailed from Spain in 1502, hopeful of obtaining in the new world the wealth and power that had somehow eluded him in the old one.

He had every reason to be confident. He was educated, cultured, and had friends and relatives with excellent social and political connections. He was a successful businessman, a singer of romances, an accomplished horseman, and an expert in the use of the sword and the lance.

In 1508, a royal patent issued by the Spanish Crown granted Nicuesa the right to conquer, colonize and govern the province of Veragua, which extended from Honduras to the Gulf of Urubá in Colombia. The following year, Nicuesa left Hispaniola in command of a fleet of 12 ships and 785 soldiers.

Nicuesa turned out to be a poor military leader. He became an arrogant and capricious dictator. He insulted his officers, refused to heed the council of his advisors, and contradicted the conclusions of his pilots.

The expedition was a disaster. Seven hundred fifteen of the

original volunteers lost their lives to tropical diseases, starvation, and the poison arrows of hostile natives. The seventy survivors, including Guerrero and Aguilar, returned with Nicuesa to the relative safety of Santa Maria de la Antigua, the Spanish settlement in Panamá that had been founded by Nicuesa, but that was now under the control of Vasco Nuñez de Balboa, the man who would later be credited with the discovery of the Pacific Ocean.

Nicuesa announced that he was reassuming his position as leader of the colony, and that he intended to take possession of the gold that had been amassed by the colonists.

Balboa refused to step down. Nicuesa was outraged. He viewed Balboa as a social inferior and a rebellious upstart.

Balboa had come from a poor family in Spain and was not formally educated. When he arrived in Hispaniola, he acquired some land and became a pig farmer. The business failed and Balboa went into debt. He had tried to ship out with Nicuesa on the ill-fated expedition, but was refused, due to his status as a debtor.

Subsequently, Balboa stowed away on a ship. He gradually achieved power and prestige and had been elected mayor of Santa Maria de la Antigua in Nicuesa's absence.

Nicuesa lacked the power to oppose the popular Balboa and was sent back to Hispaniola aboard an ill-fitted and poorly provisioned vessel under the command of a Captain Valdivia. Aguilar and Guerrero were among the twenty people aboard.

The year was 1511.

The voyage back to Hispaniola began under clear skies and over calm seas, but as the ship was sailing off the southern coast of Jamaica, the weather deteriorated and the vessel was driven onto a reef and destroyed.

The occupants managed to board the ship's boat, whereupon they drifted at the mercy of the wind and waves for thirteen days without food or water. Seven of them, including Nicuesa, died of hunger, thirst and exposure.

At long last, the thirteen shipwrecked adventurers made landfall on the coast of the Yucatán Peninsula. This was the first time that Europeans had ever set foot in what is now the nation of Mexico.

Within hours of their landing, the battered and weary castaways were captured by indigenous warriors, brought to their village and imprisoned in a cage made out of wooden sticks.

Two days later, Captain Valdivia and four other Spanish captives were killed in a ritual of human sacrifice in which the hearts were torn out of their living bodies and then eaten by the high priests and chief warriors.

The survivors knew that their time was short, and fashioned a desperate plan to escape. The eight captives called upon all their strength, pushing in unison against the thinnest sticks from which their makeshift jail had been fabricated. Finally enough branches gave way, leaving a hole through which they were able crawl out, one by one.

Slipping into the darkness, they followed one of the many roads leading out of the city. The road was bordered by an impenetrable jungle where fierce jaguars hunted their prey by night and poisonous snakes slithered in the thick bush.

At daybreak, the fugitives came to the outskirts of the city-state of Xaman Ha. Upon making contact with the natives, the Spaniards were brought before the Mayan authorities, who decided that the strangers would be granted sanctuary and would be allowed to live in the city, but only as slaves.

Within a year, the grueling work and the meager rations had claimed the lives of all but two of the Spanish adventurers, the soldier and the priest, Gonzalo Guerrero and Jerónimo de Aguilar.

From this point, the lives of these two young men were to take dramatically different paths.

Guerrero and Aguilar were sent to the city of Chetumal to be the slaves of the *cacique* (chief), Nachan Caan.

By this time, both Europeans had learned to speak the Mayan language and each, in their own different way, had begun a process of adaptation and an acceptance of their fate.

Guerrero joined Nachan Caan's army, where he quickly rose in rank and social standing, adopting Mayan customs and values. In 1514 he was granted his freedom; and, in 1516, Guerrero married the cacique's daughter and ascended to the position of *Nacon,* or General of the Army.

A year after his marriage to the Mayan princess, Guerrero set out on a road from which there was no return. According to Fray Diego de Landa in his *Relacion de las cosas de Yucatán,* written in 1565, "Guerrero taught the Indians to fight, showing them how to construct forts and bastions....He tattooed his body and let his hair grow...and he pierced his ears and lower lip in order to wear rings there...and it is probable that he became an idolater like the Maya."

Much of what we know about early Mexican history and Mayan culture comes from the writings of Fray Diego de Landa, a Franciscan priest and religious zealot who conducted an inquisition in which hundreds of Mayans were mercilessly tortured in order make them confess to their sins of idolatry and blasphemy. He also collected the many Mayan books representing all of their scientific, philosophical and metaphysical knowledge and burned them in the main plaza of the town of Mani because they were "the lies of the devil."

That year, the Spanish conquistador, Fernando Hernández de Córdoba, landed at Cape Catoche on the northeastern tip of the Yucatán Peninsula.

The Mayans, feigning friendship, signaled the Spaniards to follow them. The conquistadors were led into an ambush. Fifteen soldiers were wounded, two of whom died some days later.

The Spaniards were able to take two Mayan prisoners, who were later baptized and given the names Melchorejo and Julianillo.

Hernández de Córdoba and his soldiers then sailed west into

the Gulf of Mexico to the city of Campeche, where they were given a serious warning. According to Bernal Díaz de Castillo, one of the soldiers on the landing party:

> We went ashore near the town, which is called Campeche, where there was a pool of good water, for as far as we had seen there were no rivers in this country. We landed the casks, intending to fill them with water, and return to our ships. When the casks were full, and we were ready to embark, a company of about fifty Indians, clad in good cotton mantles, came out in a peaceful manner from the town, and asked us by signs what it was we were looking for, and we gave them to understand that we had come for water, and wished to return at once to our ships. They then made signs with their hands to find out whether we came from the direction of the sunrise, repeating the word 'Castilan, Castilan' and we did not understand what they meant by Castilan. They then asked us by signs to go with them to their town, and we decided to go with them, keeping well on the alert and in good formation. They led us to some large houses very well built of masonry, which were the Temples of their Idols and on the walls were figured the bodies of many great serpents and other pictures of evil-looking Idols. These walls surrounded a sort of Altar covered with dried blood. On the other side of the Idols were symbols like crosses, and all were coloured. At all this we stood wondering, as they were things never seen or heard of before.

> It seemed as though certain Indians had just offered sacrifices to their Idols so as to ensure victory over us. However, many Indian women moved about us, laughing, and with every appearance of good will, but the Indians gathered in such numbers that we began to fear that there might be some trap set for us, as at Catoche. While this was happening, many other Indians approached us, wearing very ragged mantles and carrying dry reeds, which they deposited on

the plain, and behind them came two squadrons of Indian archers in cotton armour, carrying lances and shields, slings and stones, and each captain drew up his squadron at a short distance from where we stood. At that moment, there sallied from another house, which was an oratory of their Idols, ten Indians clad in long white cotton cloaks, reaching to their feet, and with their long hair reeking with blood, and so matted together, that it could never be parted or even combed out again, unless it were cut. These were the priests of the Idols, and they brought us incense of a sort of resin which they call copal, and with pottery braziers full of live coals, they began to fumigate us, and by signs they made us understand that we should quit their land before the firewood which they had piled up there should burn out, otherwise they would attack us and kill us. After ordering fire to be put to the reeds, the priests withdrew without further speech. Then the warriors who were drawn up in battle array began to whistle and sound their trumpets and drums. When we perceived their menacing appearance and saw great squadrons of Indians bearing down on us we remembered that we had not yet recovered from the wounds received at Cape Catoche, and had been obliged to throw overboard the bodies of two soldiers, who had died, and fear fell on us, so we determined to retreat to the coast in good order.

The Spaniards set sail, but they were still in need of water. They dropped anchor about four miles off the coast of the town of Champotón and went ashore in their longboats.

Unbeknownst to the sailors, Gonzalo Guerrero, in his capacity of Nacon, had warned the Mayans that the Spanish were already in Cuba and that they would probably soon arrive in Mexico. He also told his adopted people of the Spanish propensity for doing harm to the indigenous inhabitants of these lands. It was Guerrero who had ordered the attack at Cape Catoche and the sign-language warning at Campeche, and it would be Guerrero who would lead the Mayans against Hernández de Córdoba and his army in the decisive battle to be fought at Champotón.

This encounter was described by Díaz del Castillo:

> As we were filling our casks with water there came along the coast towards us many squadrons of Indians clad in cotton armour reaching to the knees, and armed with bows and arrows, lances and shields, and swords like two handed broad swords, and slings and stones and carrying the feathered crests, which they are accustomed to wear. Their faces were painted black and white, and ruddled and they came in silence straight towards us, as though they came in peace, and by signs they asked whether we came from where the sun rose, and we replied that we did come from the direction of the sunrise. We were at our wits' end considering the matter, and wondering what the words were which the Indians called out to us for they were the same as those used by the people of Campeche, but we never made out what it was that they said.

> All this happened about the time of the Ave Maria, and the Indians then went off to some villages in the neighbourhood, and we posted watchmen and sentinels for security.

> While we were keeping watch during the night we heard a great squadron of Indian warriors approaching from the town and from the farms, and we knew well, that their assembly boded us no good, and we took counsel together as to what should be done. However, some said one thing and some said another. While we were still taking counsel and the dawn broke, we could see that there were about two hundred Indians to every one of us, and we said one to the other "let us strengthen our hearts for the fight, and after commending ourselves to God let us do our best to save our lives."

As soon as it was daylight we could see, coming along the coast, many more Indian warriors with their banners raised. When their squadrons were formed up they surrounded us on all sides and poured in such showers of arrows and darts, and stones thrown from their slings that over eighty of us soldiers were wounded, and they attacked us hand to hand, some with lances and the others shooting arrows, and others with two-handed knife edged swords, and they brought us to a bad pass. At last feeling the effects of our sword play they drew back a little, but it was not far, and only enabled them to shoot their stones and darts at us with greater safety to themselves.

While the battle was raging the Indians called to one another in their language "al Calachuni, Calachuni," which means "let us attack the Captain and kill him," and ten times they wounded him with their arrows; and me they struck thrice one arrow wounding me dangerously in the left side, piercing through the ribs. All the other soldiers were wounded by spear thrusts and two of them were carried off alive.

Our captain then saw that our good fighting availed us nothing; other squadrons of warriors were approaching us fresh from the town, bringing food and drink with them and a large supply of arrows. All our soldiers were wounded with two or three arrow wounds, three of them had their throats pierced by lance thrusts, our captain was bleeding from many wounds and already fifty of the soldiers were lying dead.

Feeling that our strength was exhausted we determined with stout hearts to break through the battalions surrounding us and seek shelter in the boats which awaited us near the shore; so we formed in close array and broke through the enemy.

Ah! Then to hear the yells, hisses and cries, as the enemy

showered arrows on us and hurled lances with all their might, wounding us sorely.

Then another danger befell us; as we all sought shelter in the boats at the same time they began to sink, so in the best way we could manage – hanging on to the waterlogged boats and half swimming, we reached the vessel of lightest draught which came in haste to our assistance.

Many of us were wounded while we embarked, especially those who were sitting in the stern of the boats, for the Indians shot at them as targets, and even waded into the sea with their lances and attacked us with all their strength. Thank God! By a great effort we escaped with our lives from the clutches of those people.

Within a few days we had to cast into the sea five others who died of their wounds and of the great thirst which we suffered. The whole of the fighting occupied only one hour.

After the battle of Champotón, the Spaniards left the Yucatán and returned to Cuba. Córdoba, who was wounded, died ten days later. Bernal Díaz de Castillo fully recovered from his wounds.

Unlike Guerrero, Jerónimo Aguilar remained faithful to Christianity and to Spain. When Nachan Caan offered to help Aguilar find a wife, the priest told the cacique that he could not renounce the vows of chastity he had taken. This was not in the Mayan tradition at all, and the cacique could not fathom the concept. He could not believe that a healthy man would reject a beautiful woman. On several occasions, the cacique placed Aguilar in situations where he would be alone with a woman who would make no secret of her availability.

Aguilar, however, consistently refused to give in to temptation, and the cacique finally accepted the reality of the priest's unusual philosophy. As a result, Nachan Caan awarded Aguilar the position of guardian of his harem.

In the spring of 1519, an expedition led by Hernán Cortés, consisting of eleven ships, set sail from Cuba bound for the Yucatán. On board were 508 soldiers, including 32 crossbowmen and 13 musketeers. In addition to the soldiers, there were shipmasters, pilots and sailors, numbering about one hundred. Also aboard were 16 horses, several pieces of artillery, and an ample supply of powder and shot.

Cortés landed on the island of Cozumel, a Mayan trading and religious center, off the Yucatán coast. It was here that he learned of the existence in the Yucatán of two of his countrymen. Bernal Díaz del Castillo had sailed with Cortés, and in his memoirs, he described the rescue of Aguilar:

> Cortés sent for me and a Biscayan named Martin Ramos, and asked us what we thought about those words which the Indians of Campeche had used when we went there with Fransisco Hernández de Córdoba, when they cried out "Castilan, Castilan." We again related to Cortés all that we had seen and heard about the matter, and he said that he also had often thought about it, and that perhaps there might be some Spaniards living in the country, and added "It seems to me that it would be well to ask these Caciques of Cozumel if they know anything about them." So through Melchorejo, who already understood a little Spanish and knew the language of Cozumel very well, all the chiefs were questioned, and every one of them said that they had known of certain Spaniards and gave descriptions of them, and said that some Caciques, who lived about two days' journey inland, kept them as slaves. We were all delighted at this news, and Cortés

told the Caciques that they must go at once and summon the Spaniards, taking with them letters. The Cacique advised Cortés to send a ransom to the owners who held these men as slaves, so that they should be allowed to come, and Cortés did so, and gave to the messengers all manner of beads. Then he ordered the two smallest vessels to be got ready, under the command of Diego de Ordas, and he sent them off to the coast near Cape Catoche where the larger vessel was to wait for eight days while the smaller vessel should go backwards and forwards and bring news of what was being done, for the land of Cape Catoche was only four leagues distant. In two days the letters were delivered to a Spaniard named Jerónimo de Aguilar, for that we found to be his name. When he had read the letter and received the ransom of beads which we had sent to him he was delighted, and carried the ransom to the Cacique his master, and begged leave to depart, and the Cacique at once gave him leave to go wherever he pleased. Aguilar set out for the place, five leagues distant, where his companion Gonzalo Guerrero was living, but when he read the letter to him he answered: "Brother Aguilar, I am married and have three children and the Indians look on me as a Cacique and captain in wartime – You go, and God be with you, but I have my face tattooed and my ears pierced, what would the Spaniards say should they see me in this guise? And look how handsome these boys of mine are, for God's sake give me those green beads you have brought, and I will give the beads to them and say that my brothers have sent them from my own country." And the Indian wife of Gonzalo spoke to Aguilar in her own tongue very angrily and said to him: "What is this slave coming here for talking to my husband; go off with you, and don't trouble us with any more with words." When Jerónimo de Aguilar saw that Gonzalo would not accompany him, he went at once with the two Indian messengers to the place where the ship had been awaiting his coming, but when he arrived he saw no ship, for she had already departed. The eight days during which Ordas had been ordered to await and one day more had already expired, and seeing that Aguilar had not arrived Ordas returned to Cozumel without bringing any news about that for which he had come.

When Aguilar saw that there was no ship there, he became very sad, and returned to his master and to the town where he usually lived.

When Cortés saw Ordas return without success or any news of the Spaniards or Indian messengers, he was very angry, and said haughtily to Ordas that he thought that he would have done better than to return without the Spaniards or any news of them, for it was quite clear that they were prisoners in that country.

We embarked again, and set sail on a day in the month of March, 1519 and went on our way in fair weather. At ten o'clock that same morning loud shouts were given from one of the ships, which tried to lay to, and fired a shot so that all the vessels of the fleet might hear it, and when Cortés heard this he at once checked the flagship and seeing the ship commanded by Juan de Escalante bearing away and returning towards Cozumel, he cried out to the other ships which were near him: "What is the matter? What is the matter?" And a soldier named Luis de Zaragoza answered that Juan de Escalante's ship with all the Cassava bread on board was sinking, and Cortés cried, "Pray God that we suffer no such disaster," and he ordered the Pilot Alaminos to make signal to all the other ships to return to Cozumel.

When the Spaniard who was a prisoner among the Indians, knew for certain that we had returned to Cozumel with the ships, he was very joyful and gave thanks to God, and he came in all haste with the two Indians who had carried the letters and ransom, and as he was able to pay well with the green beads we had sent him, he soon hired a canoe and six Indian rowers.

When they arrived on the coast of Cozumel and were disembarking, some soldiers who had gone out hunting (for there were wild pigs on the island) told Cortés that a large canoe, which had come from the direction of Cape Catoche, had arrived near the town. Cortés sent Andres de Tapia and two other soldiers to go and see, for it was a new thing for Indians to come fearlessly in large canoes into our neighbourhood. When Andres de Tapia saw that they were only Indians, he at once sent word to Cortés by a Spaniard that they were Cozumel Indians who had come in the canoe. As soon as the men had landed, one of them in words badly articulated and worse pronounced, cried Dios y Santa Maria de Sevilla, and Tapia went at once to embrace him.

Tapia soon brought the Spaniard to Cortés but before he arrived where Cortés was standing, several Spaniards asked Tapia where the Spaniard was. Although he was walking by his side, for they could not distinguish him from an Indian, as he was naturally brown and he had his hair shorn like an Indian slave, and carried a paddle on his shoulder, he was shod with one old sandal and the other was tied to his belt, he had on a ragged old cloak, and a worse loin cloth, with which he covered his nakedness, and he had tied up, in a bundle in his cloak, a Book of Hours, old and worn. When Cortés saw him in this state, he too was deceived like the other soldiers, and asked Tapia: "Where is the Spaniard?" On hearing this, the Spaniard squatted down on his haunches as the Indians do and said, "I am he." Cortés at once ordered him to be given a shirt and doublet and drawers and a cape and sandals, for he had no other clothes, and asked him about himself and what his name was and when he came to this country. The man replied, pronouncing with difficulty, that he was called Jerónimo de Aguilar, a native of Ecija ...

When questioned about Gonzalo Guerrero, he said that he was married and had three sons and that his ears and lower lip were pierced, that he was a seaman and a native of Palos, and that the Indians considered him to be very valiant; a little more than a year ago a captain and three vessels arrived at Cape Catoche, it was at the suggestion of Guerrero that the Indians attacked them, and that he was there in the company of the Cacique of the large town. When Cortés heard this he exclaimed, "I wish I had him in my hands; it will never do to leave him here."

Cortés and his small army went on to conquer the Aztecs, a thousand-year-old civilization, with a population of millions. There were many factors contributing to this amazing feat, but of great importance was Cortés's ability to communicate with the Aztecs in order to exploit their weaknesses. Jerónimo de Aguilar made this possible.

Aguilar joined Cortés and served as his interpreter. Julianillo and Melchorejo were no longer available. Julianillo had died and Melchorejo had escaped. Because they were being held against their will in the first place, Cortés knew he could never really rely on them, anyway. Aguilar could be trusted to communicate properly, but although he was fluent in the Mayan language, he could not speak the language of the Aztecs.

This situation was soon to change. As Cortés advanced through the Mayan territory, many Mayan leaders found it expedient to avoid direct confrontation with the well-armed Spaniards.

One of these leaders was the cacique of Tabasco. In order to appease Cortés, he gave him a gift of twenty women. One of the women, known as *La Malaniche,* was very beautiful, and Cortés took her for his mistress.

La Malaniche turned out to be the daughter of an Aztec chief, who had died when she was still a young girl. Her mother had remarried and given birth to a son.

La Malaniche's stepfather wanted his son to inherit the title of chief. In order to accomplish this, he needed to get rid of his stepdaughter, which he did by selling her to some passing traders. They eventually turned her over to the cacique of Tabasco.

La Malaniche, whose first language was Aztec, learned to speak Mayan. Now, through her, Cortés had the means to communicate with the Aztecs. He could speak to Aguilar in Spanish, Aguilar could speak to La Malaniche in Mayan, and she could then translate Cortés's words into Aztec.

Spanish hostilities against the Maya began in earnest around 1529, about ten years after Aguilar had left with Cortés. One of Cortés's lieutenants, Francisco de Montejo, was granted a

Although Jerónimo de Aguilar is revered for his dedication to his religion and his resistance to temptation, the historian Jim Tuck relates an item in the *Diccionario Porrua,* indicating that Aguilar's dedication to chastity may not have been that long-lived. He is reported to have "formed an attachment" with an Indian woman named Elvira Toznenetzin. They allegedly had two daughters and in 1526, Aguilar was awarded a grant of property in the Valley of Mexico. On his death, probably in 1531, the land reverted to the Crown. Because of his ecclesiastical status, he was ruled to have no legitimate heirs.

license from the crown to conquer the Mayans in the Yucatán.

Montejo sent a message to Guerrero asking for his help in the planned conquest.

Montejo's Message to Guerrero

Gonzalo, my brother and special mend, I count it my good fortune that I have arrived and learned of you...and you have a great opportunity to serve God and the emperor, Our Lord, in the pacification and baptism of these people, and more than this, to leave your sins behind you with the grace of God and to honor and benefit yourself. And thus I beseech you not to let the Devil influence you not to do what I say, so that he will not possess of you forever. Consequently I beseech you to come to this ship...without delay, to do what I have said and to help me carry out, through giving me your council and opinions, that which seems most expedient.

(Fernandez de Oviedo 1535)

Guerrero's answer was written on the back of the message with a piece of charcoal: "Sir, I kiss your honor's hand, but as I am a slave, I have no freedom, even though I am married and have children. And I remember God, and you, Sir, and the Spaniards, and am your good friend."

Whether or not Guerrero was indeed Montejo's "good friend" is debatable, as there is strong evidence that Guerrero was in command of the Mayan forces that opposed Montejo's military incursions.

Montejo maintained that he found Chetumal fortified, and that the Mayans used guerrilla tactics, such as digging holes along the paths leading to the city and then covering them with brush to hide them in order to trip the soldiers' horses.

According to Robert Chamberlain in his book, *Conquista y Colonización de Yucatán 1517-1550*, Montejo also asserted that "the Indians of Chetumal were numerous and hostile and cleverly guided by a renegade that knew the Spaniards and their methods of warfare."

Gonzalo Guerrero died at about the age of fifty defending his adopted homeland.

Andres de Cerezada, the royal accountant of Honduras, wrote in a report of a battle fought in Puerto Caballos on August 13, 1536, that:

> ...the cacique Cicumba, declared that during the combat a Christian Spaniard named Gonzalo had been killed by a shotgun blast. He is the one who lived among the Indians of the province of Yucatán for 20 years or more, and in addition is the one whom they say brought to ruin the commander Montejo. And when Yucatán had been abandoned by the Christians, he came with a fleet of fifty canoes to aid the natives of this province to destroy those of us who were here....This Spaniard who was killed was nude, his body decorated with tattoos, and adorned in the style of the Mayans.

Although Guerrero is considered a hero in Mexico, in Spain he was branded as a traitor to his country, to his race and to the Christian religion.

Also according to the chronicler, Oviedo: "The evil Guerrero was brought up among low and vile people, and one who was not properly instructed in the elements of our Holy Catholic Faith, or who was of low race and suspect of not being of the Christian religion."

Today, most of the population of Mexico is of mixed heritage. The children of Gonzalo Guerrero and his Mayan wife were the first Mexicans with this bloodline. A statue erected on the beach in Cozumel honors Gonzalo Guerrero as *el padre de la raza*, the father of the race.

Note: The account of the conquistador Bernal Díaz del Castillo was taken from the book, The Discovery and Conquest of Mexico 1517-1521 *by Irving A. Leonard, which was translated from the only exact copy of the original manuscript.*

IN THE EYE OF THE STORM

BY ANDREW RUTNIK

September 1995 started out with the momentous march of Hurricane Luis. Day-by-day monitoring of the weather channel showed a monster hurricane emerging. It was large, powerful and extremely dangerous. Tracking right toward us, it became the talk of the island: "Will it hit? If so, when?" and, "Have you boarded up yet?"

Luis became a Category Four when he first smashed across Antigua, leaving a trail of destruction in his wake. The 140-mile-wide eye, like a huge blender, was a day away, and heading straight for St. John. Those who hadn't boarded up, did now. I bought the last of the half-inch plywood on St. John and spent the day sealing up the house. Having gone through Hugo, my family knew what to expect. My wife, Janet, and our teenage daughter, Sophie, were busy packing up all of our favorite photographs, clothing and personal effects. These were then stored in the first floor hurricane headquarters. All the openings to our all-concrete shelter were boarded up tight except for one small door left to the outside for emergency purposes. It was as secure as you can get against the power of the angry wind.

As Labor Day weekend began, weather channels showed a high probability of a direct strike in six to twelve hours. This rapidly intensifying storm was crashing and destroying all in its path as it slammed through the Leeward Islands.

We hurried our final preparations, hindered by an unannounced power outage five hours prior to the storm's expected arrival, listening to radio reports, storm coordinates, and our governor telling us: "Prepare, pray, and good luck!"

Forced to use a handsaw, I completed all my last-minute preparations to a chorus of cursing the Water and Power Authority for shutting down before the first winds blew. Scared now, I double-boarded all my shutters, nailed up anything on the farm made of wood, took a last good look at the way it was, and sat down to stewed chicken, a meal to strengthen you through the night. Just before dark (no power), we hurriedly made last-minute provisioning of our downstairs bunker – cold water, candy, wine, Scotch, etc.

Nighttime hurricanes are like sneak attacks. The sunset is usually dramatic, a stiffening breeze pleasantly blows, but as the sky darkens, the wind increases, and the roar begins.

We were comfortably holed up, listening to radio reports, more messages of warning and preparation from our governor as we nibbled candy bars.

As midnight arrived, outside was dangerous. Trees shook from the savage gusts, branches cracked and crashed to the ground. We listened from inside as the fierce winds made low moans that would strengthen and rush up the valley in a thundering roar like a freight train rolling by, only to be followed by another, and so the night went.

Sometime in the middle of the night, Luis heeded the many prayers of Virgin Islanders and turned north, missing us by a mere 60 miles, its full force shredding St. Maarten, St. Barths and Anguilla before tracking into the North Atlantic. The damage in the Virgin Islands was minimal, the cleanup mostly trees, some roofs, poles and wires; no power, no cable, no phone.

In the days following Luis, we attempted to restore normalcy by unpacking foodstuffs, taking down some boards, cleaning up the nursery, and cussing WAPA. Radio reports told of another tropical storm (35-mph winds) by the Hollywood name of Marilyn, forming east of the Lesser Antilles. The anticlimactic effects of powerful Luis, and the location and direction of Marilyn, didn't worry many in the Virgin Islands, so life went on as usual. By the following weekend, I had all my lumber down and had paneled part of my office with the half-inch plywood. Later radio reports of Marilyn had her at about 75 to 100 mph (Category One) and going south of us, with little or no effects to be felt in the Virgin Islands.

Finally, the power came back on, phones worked, cable still out, everyone just working out of their killer storm Luis fears, looking forward to a relaxing weekend. Early Thursday radio reports had Marilyn slowing up, turning north and strengthening. Still a small hurricane – 30-mile-wide eye, 75-100 mph sustained winds, gusts up to 115 mph, only a hundred miles wide, with the worst winds in the northeast quadrant.

Everyone is shocked – what to do? We can't believe our ears. A hurricane watch for the Virgin Islands late Thursday. The Governor says to prepare – storm not as bad as Luis, but prepare. Radio reports have landfall on St. Croix by Friday morning. I rush to find plywood; everyone's out, the truck breaks down and I have to borrow one from a friend. Fortunately, Janet hadn't had time to unpack all of her Luis preparations, which were still secure, but I've got to find plywood – time is running out.

Finally as Marilyn approaches St. Croix, I find some plywood that a friend doesn't want to put up, expecting a small hurricane, and he sells it to me cheap. Janet and I are in constant contact, rushing to stores for remembered necessities. Sophie calmly helps me board up downstairs. My enthusiasm for this task is mild, because of reports of a not so dangerous hurricane, high winds in only a 30-mile-wide eye. My four-step approach to boarding up was influenced by two-hour updates, and the need to maintain comfort in our close quarters. I planned to board up if and when it was needed. Janet was anxious, pushing me to board up now – "Don't wait until the last minute..." – but I resisted, preferring to keep the steady watch as the captain of the ship. Well aware of the threat, but not too concerned, Sophie played her favorite game, Telephone.

St. Croix began feeling the feeder bands of Marilyn Friday morning. Fifty miles south of us, they were getting small gusts and showers. As the day progressed, I was into Phase Three of boarding and had Sophie holding the shutters closed while

I nailed them shut. Part of my unwillingness to board up was that each time, I put more nail holes in my windows and door casings – beautiful hardwoods from Brazil. But a knot of fear starts to build in your stomach, your adrenaline takes over, your mind races, your body tries to keep up; you stub your toe, cut your finger, bang your shin, and Phase Three is underway. Janet cooks the hurricane meal; Sophie lives in fear that I will accidentally nail her to the house. Again it's a sneak attack, a nighttime horror on its way, the sun sets, and we bunker up again.

Reports from St. Croix are not good! The lieutenant governor and his emergency team are in a National Guard bunker giving scratchy radio reports of flooding, high winds and damage. Suddenly his broadcasts are interrupted, followed by station static, and then a weak voice saying, "There goes the roof." No more St. Croix reports, the eye reportedly over southeast St. Croix, winds are definitely picking up here on St. John, we are 40 miles north and two hours away from the eye. I worry about my preparations – less than for Luis, but enough for Marilyn?

By 10:00 p.m., we were getting hit by very strong gusts – 75 to 100 mph, lots of horizontal rain, lightning, and a steady, jet-engine-like roar. My Phase Four of the plan called for doubling up shutter boards, boarding ventilation windows at either end of the bunker, and covering the remaining small door opening with anything that worked. By 11:00 p.m., screens blew out of the ventilation windows and Phase Four began. St. Thomas radio went off the air, no more reports, just us and the storm. Janet and I took wood, nails and flashlights. Scared and trembling, we ventured out to close the openings. The darkness was interrupted by flashes of lightning, silhouetting the ravished flora, starkly outlining the buildings, and quickly plunging into darkness. Hurricanes send galvanized roofing sheets flying through the air like giant razor blades; boards become missiles, walls become dangerous wafers hurtling wildly, and in the darkness where too much sound makes no sound, your instincts take over. Forcing Janet to go out into this was not easy, but as the wind and debris blew into our bunker, choices turned into action, and we crawled along the foundation and nailed shut the windows.

We found a radio station in Puerto Rico that was still broadcasting weather updates and had the storm going past us and Puerto Rico by midnight. This is where all the weather report controversy began. The first hint of something wrong in our weather updates was that our local radio station was monitoring the wind speeds – 140-mph gusts, barometric pressure approaching very close to that of the eye itself, and frantic phone calls from listeners talking about massive destruction. They were giving different wind direction reports, different wind intensity measurements, and reports of severe damage, all before midnight.

Our own experience with determining where Marilyn was happened just after midnight, when a large gust and a cracking sound sent us upstairs to see what had given way. With me in the lead, we climbed our outside stairway against a fierce wind and stinging rain. Our French doors had broken their boards and were flapping open. The pressure inside the house forced out the doors. We were near the eye. Communication had to be by instinct, because we couldn't hear each other, even at distances of one foot. Screaming did not work; 27 years of marriage did. We got the job done.

As we retreated to our downstairs haven, the lightning flashes revealed a destroyed landscape. Our buildings still stood, but our fears intensified. With Sophie asleep and Janet exhausted by our ordeal, I opened the Scotch and stood guard against Marilyn. Sometime around 1:00 a.m., it calmed. Thinking the storm had passed, I went out with a flashlight to inspect our home and nursery. Stripped trees, downed greenhouses, blown roof parts, a chaotic mess littered the landscape. Within five minutes the storm came back, shaking me out of sadness, sending me running for the bunker.

The Puerto Rico radio station meteorologist was now openly contradicting the National Weather Service tracking reports. Claiming access to the same hurricane-hunter airplane information, satellite photos, and local monitoring reports, he had the eye over St. John at this time. He was right. The second half of this hurricane was now blasting us. It was stronger, louder and more frightening than anyone can imagine. In my run to the bunker, I was assaulted by jet-airplane blasts that tore through the nursery. I dodged branches and got plastered with spinach-like shredded leaves. When I finally got back inside, I was shaking with fear. I prayed that our home would not blow away.

A feeling of doom settles in when you realize how weak you are compared to what's happening outside. I sat on the couch listening to Marilyn lay down her fury, fighting those winds with gritting teeth, as if my spirit alone could hold the house together.

Sometime around 5:00 a.m., I was startled by a bang at the door. In the darkness I saw two young ladies illuminated by flashes of lightning. As I opened the door, their cries of relief at finding a safe haven, and the condition of their clothing, shocked me out of my gloomy daze. Dawn approached and Marilyn blew herself out. We huddled together as the first rays of light revealed the devastated landscape. After some much-needed hot tea, clean clothes, and bandages, the two young ladies related their own hurricane tale.

Having rented a small house above ours facing beautiful Reef Bay, they had planned on just relaxing on St. John. The rental agent advised them that a tropical storm or a small hurricane could approach our area soon. They prepared by getting flashlights ready, good books and a six-pack of Heineken.

With the first big winds of Marilyn, around 10:15 p.m., the main roof blew off, and glass was flying everywhere. By 10:30, they had retreated to the last standing room, a laundry room. Minutes later, the walls came crashing down as they huddled at the base of a washing machine. Saved by that machine from being crushed by a falling wall, they sought to escape through a window with a 10-foot drop. Landing in scrubby thorny bush, they crawled off into the dark night over sharp rocks and broken trees. Finally, far enough away from the crashing house, they dug holes with their manicured fingernails and lay down beside a fallen tree for six hours to watch the Marilyn show on the big screen in the sky.

They decided to look for shelter and set out into the darkness. Trying to remember where they saw houses on their earlier trip to the beach, they headed down the road littered with downed power lines, trees, rockslides and other debris. The first house they came to was flattened – refrigerators lying in the road, furniture scattered everywhere, no signs of people. Eventually they ended up at our bunker room, scratched, punctured and shocked by what they had just experienced.

As the morning progressed, squalls of rain and wind were all that remained of Marilyn's power. We were exhausted and in a state of shock, trying to calm our ragged nerves and reconcile ourselves to what had happened.

Voices of neighborhood search parties could be heard, noisy chainsaws opening roads.

"You guys all right?" they called out.

Joining the group, we heard of harrowing rescues, collapsed houses, missing people, a seriously injured couple, and frightening individual tales of escapes in mid-storm from collapsing houses.

As the hours and days after the storm rolled by, we adjusted to the survival struggle. Post-hurricane weather is always muggy, hot and windless. The trees are stripped of vegetation and provide no shelter from the tropical sun. Cold water is nonexistent, ice only a fantasy, and electric fans two months away.

Our two visitors were healed enough to venture into town and seek help and evacuation assistance from the Red Cross. We bade them goodbye, wished them luck (because that's what it would take to get out), and assured them St. John would be back.

To end this story, I think a couple of unusual observations are in order. First, imagine a whole house blown away except for one wall. On that wall was a painting, framed in glass, virtually unaffected by the 150-mph winds that blew away the rest of the house. Second, a 30' by 50' house, glass doors, louvered windows, wood construction, picked up and moved 60 feet from its foundation, with not a window, glass door, or piece of wood broken or cracked.

"Thank God for life," was the constant refrain coming from all quarters: high and low, rich and poor, black and white, hugging in the street, happy to be alive.

PIRATE BIRTHDAY PARTY

BY GERALD SINGER

Romanticized tales of pirates and buried treasure have long been an integral part of West Indian folklore, capturing the imagination of both young and old. Former St. John residents John and Jennifer Campbell and their children were no exceptions. They loved to read and listen to stories about the pirates that terrorized the Caribbean in the old colonial days.

Some years ago when Ross, one of the Campbell children, was about to celebrate his eighth birthday, John and Jennifer organized a party at the public beach at Hawksnest Bay. The theme of the party was pirates.

The adult Campbells hatched up an elaborate scheme. An authentic-looking treasure chest was made out of an old wooden box and filled with "silver and gold" (pennies and nickels) and rare spices (candies and cookies) garnered from the four corners of the globe. The pirate chest was then buried just under the surface of the sand alongside a sea grape tree.

Next, a treasure map was drawn, using paper that had been burned on the edges to make it look old and mysterious. The map contained easily followed instructions.

The pirates were recruited from among John's friends and colleagues. They wore eye patches and bandannas and carried pirate swords (machetes). A black 19-foot Zodiac inflatable boat (powered by an outboard engine) served as the pirate ship. A large Jolly Roger flag was hoisted up on a mast so that everyone would know that those on board were genuine bloodthirsty buccaneers.

When the children arrived at the beach for the birthday party, they were informed that pirates had been seen in the vicinity. If any pirates should come even near the beach, the children were instructed to run and hide as quickly as possible because pirates were, after all, dangerous fellows.

Just about an hour after the start of the party, while the children were playing on the beach, a strange craft was seen approaching Hawksnest from the north.

As it came closer, one of the children recognized the skull and crossbones of the Jolly Roger flag and correctly identified the vessel. "Pirates!" he shouted, "Hide!"

The children ran for cover under the sea grape and maho trees.

The ominous pirate boat landed on the beach and the motley

crew stepped ashore. A mean and nasty-looking swashbuckler peered up and down the beach.

"Do you see kids around?" he growled, staring at the sea grape tree under which four or five children were hiding (and spying). This was obviously too much for one little boy who darted out from under the branches and ran, screaming at the top of his lungs, to his mother who did her best to calm the young lad.

"No, no sign of kids around here," replied another pirate, gamely ignoring the sobs of the frightened child.

"Who has the map?" queried a one-eyed buccaneer. "It's right here," answered the pirate captain, who looked a little like John Campbell, but more fierce. "Let's bury it where no one will EVER find it," he said, as he hid the map under a few inches of sand, seemingly unaware that the eyes of more than a dozen children were following his every move.

With the map and treasure well hidden and the day's mission accomplished, the brigands returned to their ship. As they boarded the boat, they could a hear a tourist kid, who had been watching the drama unfold from down the beach, ask his mother, "Were those real pirates, mom?"

The pirates, employing an outboard motor instead of the more traditional sails, sped off into the boundless blue sea.

Meanwhile, with the sea dogs only a short distance offshore, one of the braver birthday party kids came out of hiding and ran to the sandy area where he had seen the pirates stash their secret treasure map.

The pirates motored around Lind Point to Cruz Bay, washed off their pirate makeup, removed their eye patches, and put away their swords. They secured the pirate ship, boarded a Nissan pickup and drove back to Hawksnest to join the birthday party.

Upon their arrival at the beach, a gaggle of excited kids surrounded the newcomers (none of whom was suspected of piracy) and regaled them with the story of their recent encounter with real Caribbean pirates, their narrow escape, and their recovery of a fabulous buried treasure.

The fact that the children believed the charade, and so wholeheartedly entered into the fantasy, made all of the elaborate preparations well worthwhile and even warmed the hearts of the cold-blooded pirates.

NORMAN ISLAND

By Gerald Singer

In the 1700s, Spanish exploration and conquest of the New World and the establishment of trade with Asia and India led to an accumulation of riches from far-flung parts of the globe. The new owners of this precious cargo then needed to transport it to Spain in as safe and reliable a manner as could be arranged in a world where ships of enemy nations, pirates, and privateers stalked the seas on the lookout for treasure-laden vessels.

The Treasure Route

In South America, gold and precious gems, stolen from sacred Inca graves or mined in forced labor camps, were brought overland to the walled city of Cartegena.

Rare and exotic spices, ivory, jade and silk were gathered in the far-off lands of Asia and the East Indies and loaded aboard galleons, which sailed across the Pacific to the port cities of Acapulco and Panamá. These items, along with other valuables, such as pearls from the Pearl Islands, were loaded onto the backs of mules and transported to the Caribbean cities of Vera Cruz or Portobello.

From Portobello, Vera Cruz and Cartegena, the treasures were shipped to the fortified city of Havana, where they were consolidated and stored, along with indigo, rum, sugar, tobacco, cochineal, quinine, coffee and cocoa from Cuba and other Caribbean islands.

When there was enough merchandise to warrant the expense, it was sent to Spain on galleons, escorted by heavily armed warships. These armadas sailed north, riding the currents of the Gulf Stream until they reached the latitudes of the prevailing westerlies, where they would then turn east and sail downwind to Spain.

THE WRECK OF *NUESTRA SEÑORA DE GUADELUPE*

In the summer of 1750, the five-hundred-ton Spanish galleon, *Nuestra Señora de Guadelupe*, commanded by Juan Manuel de Bonilla and escorted by a convoy of seven warships, left Havana harbor bound for the Spanish port city of Cadiz.

Packed away in the ship's holds was a vast fortune in gold, silver, wrought plate, indigo, cochineal and tobacco.

On August 15, 1750, while sailing through a section of the Atlantic Ocean known as the Devil's Triangle, the armada encountered a fierce tropical storm. *Nuestra Señora de Guadelupe* went aground off the island of Ocracoke in the British Colony of North Carolina. Three of her accompanying galleons disappeared in the same storm and not a trace of their wreckage has ever been found.

THE DISPUTE

When the seas calmed, the Captain General of the Province of North Carolina visited the crippled galleon. He claimed that duties were owed on the landed merchandise. Captain Bonilla disputed this claim, citing the terms of the treaty between Britain and Spain pertaining to shipping and trade. The Captain General temporarily placed the treasure in British custody and Bonilla accompanied him ashore to debate the matter.

Meanwhile, the governor of South Carolina, who had heard of the incident, sent a courier with a message to impound the *Nuestra Señora de Guadelupe* in order to settle claims made by citizens of South Carolina against the Spanish governor of Havana. It seems that the governor had illegally impounded several English ships after the conclusion of the peace treaty, and the ship owners now demanded compensation.

PIRATES STEAL THE TREASURE

During the negotiations between the governor general of North Carolina and Captain Bonilla, and while the South Carolina contingent was still en route, the treasure was stolen by pirates, who loaded the cargo onto two shallow draft sailboats called bilanders, craft designed for inland navigation only.

THE TREASURE ARRIVES IN THE VIRGIN ISLANDS

One of the heavily laden vessels promptly foundered and sank, but the other, commanded by the Englishman Owen

Lloyd, successfully sailed over 1,000 miles of ocean and made landfall on the Danish island of St. Croix.

Here, the pirates disposed of some of their money and then sailed north to Norman Island, where the chests of gold and silver were painstakingly hidden. They then set sail for St. Thomas, where they sold the cochineal, tobacco and indigo, along with the unsuitable bilander itself. After a drunken spending spree at the grog shops and brothels on the Charlotte Amalie waterfront, Lloyd and his men made their way back to St. Croix, where they bought a sloop and sailed to the British Leeward Islands.

THE RACE TO FIND THE TREASURE

The pirates' behavior on St. Croix and St. Thomas was, to say the least, indiscreet; and as news of the stolen treasure spread, interested parties soon put two and two together and had a fair idea of the identity of the suspects and the location of the treasure.

In all probability, the pirates were observed in the vicinity of Norman Island by seamen coming in and out of the harbor at Roadtown, Tortola. Whatever the cause, a certain curiosity must have arisen concerning Norman Island, because a search party was organized to investigate. The searchers apparently included Abraham Chalwil, the president of the Council in Tortola, and other leading citizens.

At least a portion of the treasure was found on Norman Island and brought back to Tortola. The members of the expedition, however, did not relay news of the find to government officials in the Leeward Islands. They simply decided to keep what they found.

As was the case with the original pirates, the virtue of discretion was not practiced, and rumors of their find proliferated throughout the West Indies.

Meanwhile, the British and the Spanish were busily following the trail of the pirates and the treasure, which both nations now claimed as their own.

The Lieutenant Governor of Antigua, Mr. Fleming, was the first government official to take direct action. He traveled to Nevis, St. Kitts, Montserrat and Anguilla, where he disseminated information about the piracy suspects in the hope that they would be apprehended.

In Anguilla, Fleming was informed that a man who called himself Davidson had been arrested after he tried to buy provisions with a newly minted gold doubloon. He was interrogated and confessed that his real name was Blackstock and that he was, indeed, one of the pirates so eagerly sought.

The next entry into the race to find the hidden fortune would have been the Dutch governor of Sint Eustatius (Statia). The pirate leader, Owen Lloyd, had been arrested on that island and had furnished a full confession. Now the Dutch governor thought that he could go and get the treasure for himself. He was preparing to send out some soldiers to Norman Island, but before he could get the expedition underway, Governor Fleming found out about the plan. He told the Dutchman that he would confiscate any vessel and arrest its crew if anyone tried to steal the treasure that he said rightfully belonged to the British.

Fleming sailed to Tortola, where he learned that some of the inhabitants had already been to Norman Island and had brought the treasure back to Tortola. He also realized that the Tortolans, who were generally poor and had a history of being harassed by the Spanish, would be extremely reluctant to give up what they had found.

In a letter concerning the incident, Fleming wrote:

> Furnished with the confession of Blackstock, I landed at Tortola on Monday the 25 November and finding it confirmed, in every particular, I hoped the certainty it gave me as to the species and quantity of the treasure, would afford me great assistance in my inquiry, but I did not find it so. I instantly sent for the president, Abraham Chalwil, who attended me, and I had very soon a number of the best of the inhabitants about me, but they did not bring with them a disposition to acknowledge for themselves, or betray the confidences, I am told, they had entered into.

Fleming used "the carrot and stick" solution to solve the problem. He offered a large reward in the form of a one-third finder's fee for those that turned in their share. Confiscation, arrest and punishment awaited those who did not.

The president of the Council, along with several other citizens, finally acknowledged the existence and whereabouts of the treasure and at least a portion of it was returned. Chalwil, however, was to eventually lose his job over the matter.

Coins and merchandise valued at $20,429 were eventually turned in, and $7,514 of that was issued as a finder's fee.

The estimated value of the cargo originally stolen from the galleon was over $200,000; this left about $180,000 (worth millions of dollars by today's standards) still unaccounted for.

WHAT HAPPENED TO THE REST OF THE FORTUNE?

The Spanish maintained that the treasure was rightfully theirs, since they were the ones who had taken it from the Native Americans in the first place. When word spread that the *Nuestra Señora* cargo had found its way to the Virgin Islands, the governor of Puerto Rico sent soldiers to investigate, and there is evidence that they may have met with some success. This story takes us back to the island of Anegada and a man named George Norman.

Anegada never developed a significant plantation or agricultural economy, and at this time, most of the inhabitants of the island were nefarious and desperate individuals who dedicated themselves to piracy and the plunder of ships wrecked on the Anegada Horseshoe Reef.

A deed dated 1747 showed a George Norman to be the owner of over four percent of the island of Anegada. Many speculate that his money came from questionable sources:

According to George Eggleston in his book *Virgin Islands*, Norman Island "was named for a pirate skipper who had a one-man kingdom on the island and for many years preyed upon the shipping that passed through Sir Francis Drake Channel."

If George Norman had anything to do with Norman Island at the time of the piracy, he would have been among the Virgin Islanders who found portions of the loot there. He may even have been in cahoots with the pirates.

The book, *Lagooned in the Virgin Islands,* by H. B. Eadie, mentions a letter dated December 22, 1750, which refers to "troublesome Spaniards infesting the seas around the Virgin Islands" and their recovery of part of the loot from the caravel *Nuestra Señora* that had been buried at Norman Island.

In *Letters From The Virgin Islands,* written anonymously, reference is made of the Spanish recapture of the treasure: "Norman, a buccaneer, separating himself from his associates, then in force at Anegada, had settled with his portion of the general booty, on this Key...in a conflict [with the Spanish] ...Norman and his followers perished."

The next rumor of a treasure find came in the early nineteenth century after Captain Thomas Southey described Peter Island in his *Chronological History of the West Indies.* He wrote:

In May [1806] the author with a party visited Peter's Island, one of those which from the Bay of Tortola, a kind of Robinson Crusoe spot, where a man ought to be a farmer, carpenter, doctor, fisherman, planter; everything himself. The owner's house has only the ground floor; a roof of shingles projects some six or eight feet beyond the sides, like a Quaker's hat; not a pane of glass in the house; merely shutters for the apertures. In the centre of the drawing-room or hall, or best room were triced up ears of Indian corn; on a chair lay a fishing net; in one corner hung another; spyglass, a fowling piece, chairs, looking glass, and pictures of the four seasons composed the furniture; the library consisted of a prayer-book, Almanack, and one volume of the Naval Chronicle. On the left hand was a room, with a range of machines for extracting the seeds from the cotton. Round the house were abundance of goats, turkeys, fowls, a bull, cow, pigs, dogs and cats...

The Old Gentleman was dressed in a large broad-brimmed white hat which appeared to have been in use for over a century; a white night-cap covered his bald head; his blue jacket had lapels buttoned back; his duck waistcoat had flaps down to his knees; the trousers were of the same material as his waistcoat...the man leading this isolated life with only his old wife, who looked more like an Egyptian mummy than anything human, was worth £60,000...He had lived twenty years on that small island and twenty on Tortola.

The eccentric couple later went to live on Norman Island, supposedly in search of greater seclusion, but the talk was that they had returned to look for more treasure.

Thomas Southey was the brother of the well-known poet, Robert Southey, which helped give this rather obscure book a wide circulation. In conjunction with the later activities of the hermit couple, there arose a renewed interest in the lost treasure of Norman Island.

A group of English treasure hunters formed the Norman's Island Treasure Company. The adventurers sailed to Norman Island, where they set off large charges of gunpowder to blast holes in places where they thought that the loot might have been hidden. There was no record of a find, but it is said that some of these holes can be still be seen today.

Julian Putley in *The Virgin's Treasure Island* writes:

> The southernmost cave has natural steps carved into one side and it was at the top of these steps that, in 1910 or thereabouts, a treasure chest was found containing Spanish doubloons. The find was verified by a fisherman, who, whilst sheltering from the rain, found an empty iron chest and a few telltale coins.... Rumor has it that when descendants of Mr. Creque are betrothed, a Spanish doubloon hanging from a gold chain is presented to the lucky bride.

The most recent report of a treasure find on Norman Island

concerns the Creque family. Eggleston wrote: "Just after the turn of the last century an impoverished Virgin Islander named Creque made a systematic search of the caves and found the treasure chest previously mentioned. The well-heeled Creque family are prominent merchants in St. Thomas to this day."

(Mr. Creque bought Norman Island and the Creque family became significant landowners on St. Thomas and St. John. Creque's Alley in downtown Charlotte Amalie was the subject of a hit song by the Mommas and the Poppas in the 1960s.

THE PENNS

BY GERALD SINGER

In 1937, the island of Marina Cay in the British Virgin Islands was purchased by a young American couple, Robb and Rodie White, who, with the aid of some of the residents of Fat Hog Bay, Tortola, built a small home on the top of the cay's only hill.

Today, Pussers operates a small hotel, marina and restaurant on the island. The house, built by Robb and Rodie White, still stands and serves as a library and reading room.

In his book, *Two On The Isle*, Robb White recounts the couple's experiences and adventures during the three years that they lived happily and peacefully on that deserted tropical island. In 1959, the book was made into a popular motion picture entitled *Our Virgin Island*.

A major character in the book and movie was a young

Tortolan from Fat Hog Bay, described as:

...a spectacular man ... about six feet tall, with shoulders flat as planks and under the velvet black skin, muscles that looked like fluid bands. He had a gentle, sweet face and all his words sounded round...

He had become our indispensable friend and almost our only contact with the world beyond Tortola. He sailed the list of our needs down to Maurice Titley in Roadtown, and brought back the goods; he saw to it that the priceless manuscripts got aboard the once-a-week launch sailing to the nearest post office at Charlotte Amalie in St. Thomas; he brought us bundles of charcoal and choice slabs of meat whenever a cow or pig was butchered in Fat Hog Bay. He had Panama hats made for us by East End ladies standing waist deep in the sea and weaving them underwater...

One day, a 45-foot yawl dropped anchor behind the reef protecting the island, and a four-man crew of German Nazis came ashore. The sailors were threatening and abusive.

They forced their way into the house. Three of the Germans subdued Robb White while the fourth announced his intention to rape Rodie.

The Whites were saved, just in the nick of time, by their West Indian friend, who had seen the suspicious-looking yacht heading toward Marina Cay.

With cutlash in hand, the formidable Tortolan announced that he had come to inform the Germans that their yacht and dinghy were adrift and that maybe they should do something about it before their vessel drifted onto the reef.

In the movie, the Tortolan was played by Sidney Poitier. The book version used the heroic character's real name, Richard Penn, who was the real-life uncle of several prominent St. Johnians, including the three generations of Richard Penns who now live on St. John.

Photo by Gerald Singer

Richard Penn, the nephew of the Richard Penn who appears in Robb White's book. (The man in the backgound is Calis Sewer.)

The Penns of the Virgin Islands have a distinguished ancestry, being the direct descendants of the founder of Pennsylvania, William Penn.

"William Penn the Quaker was the son of Admiral Penn, who took Jamaica, West Indies, for the British Crown and who also served King Charles II in various other ways. His son, William Penn, became a Quaker, and went out into the streets with George Fox preaching the Quaker religion, which was then illegal in England, and for this, he was put into prison. At a later date, King Charles II settled the debt which he owed to Admiral Penn by granting to his son William a tract of land in North America some 300 miles long by 160 miles wide, thus discharging his debt and ridding himself of a troublesome Quaker at one and the same time.

"Thus it was that William Penn left England and, together with a few other like-minded Quakers, sailed for North America....From written sources, I later discovered how William and Benjamin, the two sons of William Penn the Quaker, came to be in Tortola. It appears that when in Boston, they became involved in a fracas one evening and deemed it prudent to leave that same night on one of the sailing ships bound for the West Indies and due to return with a cargo of sugar, molasses and rum. In any event, the brothers were never seen in Boston again and it was assumed that they arrived in Barbados with one of those ships and from there made their way to Tortola. Both written records and oral tradition agree that they first stayed on Beef Island and the Camanoes, and later crossed over to East End, where they established themselves. Local records show that the brothers owned land at East End, Greenland and the Camanoes.

"An interesting sidelight, which tends to confirm this early history, was provided by Mr. McGlynn, a graduate of the University of Pittsburgh, who spent some time in Tortola researching our old Government records. He told me that around this time, a William Penn fathered two boys by a slave owned by a Mr. Vanterpool. In order to give the children their freedom and the right to the Penn name, it was necessary for him to buy them."

Memoirs of H. R. Penn, by H.R. Penn O.B.E., 1990.

A ST. THOMAS AIRPORT STORY

By Gerald Singer

In order to fly to the United States mainland from St. Thomas, passengers must first proceed through several checkpoints. These include: ticket and boarding pass verification, customs, agriculture, immigration, the metal detector and x-ray machine at airport security, and lastly the gate agent who makes sure that no unknown persons came to your house and packed your bags for you, possibly inserting a bomb into your luggage without your knowledge.

It's all pretty routine and in most cases you are just shuffled from one station to the next without much interaction with the officials.

One day I was on my way to the mainland and found myself passing through the aforementioned gauntlet. It was the same old procedure, until I reached immigration.

I was very early for my flight and was the only person on line.

"What does the computer say about me?" I asked.

"Nothing," the immigration officer replied.

We then struck up a conversation about computers and the power that they hold. He told me that immigration had its own data bank, which was what he had just looked at. A great body of information was also available from a variety of other sources such as city and state police departments, FBI, CIA, DEA and Interpol. These databases were only supposed to be accessed if the immigration officer had some good reason to do so, or if a red flag came up indicating that one of these agencies had pertinent information on the individual in question. They were not to be called up indiscriminately.

To illustrate the point the officer told me a story that he had heard about an agent in St. Thomas who didn't follow the rules:

It seems that one day, during a particularly slow period, an immigration officer stationed at the St. Thomas Airport became bored and decided to amuse himself by looking up information on his computer.

Alleged mobster, John Gotti, had recently been in the news, and the officer, who was said to be curious about all the media attention being given to the New York City Mafia, ran Gotti's name through the computer as if he were a passenger going through immigration. I'm sure his efforts were rewarded with a cornucopia of Gotti-bits from innumerable sources, and that he was easily able to entertain himself until his next client appeared on the immigration line.

Unbeknownst to the immigration officer, at the very moment that he was playing hacker with his government-issued computer, John Gotti was the subject of a super-secret, intensive surveillance carried out by several federal government agencies acting in conjunction with the New York City Police Department. He was being tailed by teams of investigators, his phones and all the payphones in his neighborhood and in places where he was known to frequent were tapped and video cameras had been installed in several strategic areas to record his movements. The long arm of the law was closing in on the supposed "capo de tutti capos" (boss of all bosses) and the cops and government agents were just about to make the biggest collar of their careers.

As soon as Gotti's name went through the system, it was picked up by the computer geeks who were keeping a sharp electronic eye on Gotti and his movements. They couldn't believe the words that flashed across their computer monitors.

Gotti, it seemed, had slipped through the tightly woven net and had just passed through immigration at the Cyril E. King International Airport in St. Thomas. What was he doing there? And how could this have happened? Heads were going to roll.

Investigators were summarily dispatched to St. Thomas. Calls were frantically made to the chiefs of the various agencies, who filtered the shocking news down the chain of command to the operatives on the street, and the carefully thought out procedure that had been moving along without a hitch, suddenly was in a state of turmoil.

Of course all the confusion was gradually sorted out, and the Gotti bust, perhaps slightly delayed, was carried out successfully. Needless to say, the career of the curious immigration officer came to an ignominious end, but his story lives on as a stern reminder that the abuse of power doesn't come without a price.

THE XTABAY

By Gerald Singer

Once upon a time in a Mayan village, there lived two women who happened to be born at the same time and on the same day. Both of them were extremely beautiful, but one was known to give herself, body and spirit, to whatever man desired her. Because of this, she was called the Xkeban (pronounced shke-bonn), which in Mayan means "sinner, whore or giver of illicit sex." It was for this reason that many of the villagers despised her, and she was often taunted and mistreated.

But the Xkeban had a pure and noble heart. She took care of the sick and sold the jewels and finery that were given to her by her many lovers to feed the hungry. She was the only one in the village to care for animals that had been abandoned when they were no longer useful. She was loving and humble and never spoke poorly of anyone.

The other woman was pure of body and never gave herself to any man. The villagers called her the Utz-colel, which in Mayan means "virtuous, clean and decent." Because of this, she enjoyed the respect and admiration of the people.

The Utz-colel, on the other hand, was rigid and arrogant, never giving to beggars. She would point out that vagrancy was not to be encouraged. She treated the humble, the needy and the poor as weaklings and inferiors and held particular disdain for those who had committed sins of love. Illness was repugnant to her. Her heart was as cold as a dead rattlesnake.

One day, the people of the village began to notice a scent in the air. It was penetrating, yet gentle, light and pleasant. They followed the scent to the house of the Xkeban. The villagers then realized that it had been several days since anyone had seen her. They called out, and when no one answered, they opened the door and went inside. There they found the Xkeban dead, surrounded by loving and grieving animals. It was from her dead body that the divine odor was emanating.

When the news reached the Utz-colel, she at first said that the people must be lying or mistaken. She said that the effluence of a sinner would be pestilential and should be avoided. This is what she said, but being curious she went to the house of the Xkeban to find out for herself. Then, when she personally experienced the pleasant and gentle aroma, she pronounced that it was the work of evil spirits trying to seduce the men of the village. Inwardly, she thought how much better her virtuous body would smell when her time came to die.

Strangely enough, the sweet scent stayed in the air along the road leading to the cemetery for three days after the Xkeban was buried. Beautiful wildflowers grew up and covered the earth around her grave.

Exactly one year later, the Utz-colel died, certain that she would be well rewarded in the hereafter. Nevertheless, for three days after she was buried, her body gave off such a foul odor that the people of the town could not help but vomit. No one could explain how it was that all the flowers that were brought to her grave withered and died within minutes.

It was then that the people realized the truth: Real virtue comes from the heart.

They say that the Xkeban, who shared her sweetness, was changed into the white flower of the xtabentún (pronounced shta-ben-tún), a flower that, like love, intoxicates. A drink made from the nectar of this flower evokes the sensation of being held in the arms of lovely Xkeban.

The "virtuous" Utz-colel, on the other hand, turned into the flower of the tzacam, a cactus flower, reminiscent of her character: beautiful, but full of sharp spines. The flower at a distance seems odorless, but up close it emits the nauseating smell of a putrefying corpse.

The Utz-colel began to reflect on her life on Earth. She thought about the Xkeban and how she had been rewarded after death. The envious Utz-colel did not give a thought to the purity of the Xkeban's heart and spirit, but attributed the Xkeban's good fortune to her many love affairs.

The Utz-colel called out to the spirits and asked to be returned to life so that she could experience love. But her love was perverted and evil, due to the coldness of her spirit, and so it came to be that the Utz-colel returned as the dreaded Xtabay woman (pronounced shta-bye), an evil being that hides in the deep folds of the kapok tree, which the Mayans call ceiba. She takes the form of a beautiful woman, combing her long hair with cactus spines, and seduces young men, killing them in the midst of their passion.

Jesús Azcorra Alejos writes:

If, while passing this tree at night, you catch a fleeting glimpse of a beautiful woman, or if you hear a soft whispered phrase or a sweet song of love, do not look up. Avert your gaze and walk in the center of the path. Avoid the thick bush on the sides of the road from which the spirit may emerge, for if you are unfortunate enough to gaze into the eyes of this bewitching and seductive creature, she will cast a spell on you and you will be overwhelmed by love. She will beckon you to come closer and you will not be able to resist her passionate embrace, which will cause you to fall into a deep and hypnotic sleep. When you awake you will find that you have been embracing a spiny cactus and the wounds that you receive may result in a fever that is very often fatal. Beware!

The preceding story is partly a loose translation of Diez Leyendas Mayas *by Jesús Azcorra Alejos and partly anecdotal accounts that I came across while traveling in the Yucatán.*

SCHOOL BUS

BY GERALD SINGER

The easterly tradewinds blowing in from Africa first meet St. John over the long and narrow peninsula appropriately called East End. When these winds meet the higher elevations further west, the cool air currents rising from mountain slopes cause rain. Over East End, however, the trades often dry out the earth and erode the exposed hillsides. Consequently, East End is arid, rocky and rugged and cultivation of the land is difficult and unrewarding.

The first settlers on East End were poor white farmers who owned small tracts of land and had few, if any, slaves.

In 1733, the slaves on St. John revolted and took over the island. Most East End farmers abandoned their holdings and escaped by boat to St. Thomas and Tortola. Their farms reverted to bush.

After the slave revolt was put down by French troops, St. John plantations were reestablished, but this was not the case at the barren East End where the land remained vacant and was put up for sale.

Thus, slaves who had been freed by their masters and people of mixed race (known as free coloreds) could, after years of hard work and saving, afford to buy small tracts of land there.

So it came to pass that a free community was established at East End some fifty years before slavery was finally abolished on St. John.

East End had abundant marine resources, and a strong tradition of seafaring developed among the people. There were numerous protected bays from which boats could be launched or moored and where nets could be set to catch turtles and fish. Whelk could be picked along the rocky shoreline and conch harvested from shallow undersea grasslands.

The seafaring tradition was further strengthened by the quality and popularity of the boats built by East End craftsmen and by the area's unique geographical location, which made travel by sea the most convenient method of transportation.

Coral Bay, a small commercial center at the time, was accessible by land but only over a steep and rugged path. It was much easier for East Enders to row or sail to Coral Bay, and most visits there were made by boat.

Roadtown, Tortola was another common destination for East Enders who would often sail there to trade, shop or see doctors and dentists. Roadtown was less than ten miles to the north by sea, and, as the tradewinds came from the east, it was a relatively easy sail in both directions. East Enders would visit Roadtown so regularly that Saturdays became known as "St. John Day" on Tortola.

In 1863, the citizens of East End built and maintained a school that was run by the Moravian Church and supported by the Danish government. Since then, schooling and education have always been given a high priority in the East End community.

In the 1920s, Guy Benjamin, an East End native, was one of twenty-four students in attendance at the East End School. He became the first St. Johnian to graduate from the Charlotte Amalie High School in St. Thomas and later received a Bachelor of Arts degree from Howard University and a Master's degree from New York University.

Guy Benjamin returned to St. John, where he taught first at Bethany and then at the Benjamin Franklin School in Coral Bay. He taught sixth, seventh and eighth grades at Benjamin Franklin and was unofficially in charge of that school as well as the East End School. (The school was later renamed the Guy H. Benjamin School in his honor.)

The population of East End was then declining and fewer children went to the school. When one of the teachers at East End, Mrs. Fernandez, left the school, there were only eight children left. Rather than find a new teacher, it was decided that the school would be closed and the East End children would attend classes in Coral Bay.

True to East End tradition, the children were taken to school by boat. Another East Ender, Ivan George, was hired for this purpose. Every morning, Ivan rowed the schoolchildren, five of whom were his and his wife's, from Salt Well Bay in East End to Coral Bay. Then, when school was dismissed, Ivan met the children and rowed them back to East End.

The small, open rowboat was a less-than-ideal method of transportation. Adverse weather conditions often made it impossible for the children to get to school, and, most importantly, the school could not get insurance for a rowing boat.

There was, however, a man named Kendell Anthony, who would routinely negotiate the road to East End in his four-wheel-drive water truck. Guy Benjamin, sensing a solution to the transportation problem, lobbied successfully to get Mr. Anthony the contract as school bus driver.

Mr. Anthony dismantled the water tank, installed sides and seats. When the necessary insurance was granted, the eight children of isolated East End became some of the first children on St. John to ride to school in a real school bus.

THE HURRICANE

By Gerald Singer

The night was dark and forbidding and the weather was turn-ing ugly. Huge waves were battering at the sailboat; a strong gust of wind had just shredded the fully reefed mainsail. John, a Navy veteran who had spent much of his life dealing with the sea, had never seen anything like it.

At about 6:00 a.m., John saw a freighter pounding through the rough seas at top speed. Using his handheld VHF, he established contact with the ship's radio operator and asked for the latest weather update. The news was bad. John was directly in the path of an oncoming hurricane.

John had set sail two weeks before from Aruba, bound for Nassau. The voyage represented the beginning of a new life for the 50-year-old, recently retired and recently divorced American, whose children were grown up, and whose plan it was to sail around the world at his own pace and in his own style. It was also a rebirth for the boat that John was sailing, a 50-foot steel ketch, which had just been totally overhauled and lovingly refurbished and refitted.

When John had first seen the old and neglected ketch rusting at a boatyard in La Guaira, Venezuela, he immediately looked beyond its shabby appearance and focused on the basic hull design. As a past Navy man who had developed a great respect for the sea, he appreciated the boat's inherent seaworthiness: its solid steel construction and eight-and-a-half-foot deep keel. As a future cruising yachtsman, he liked the boat's wide 15-foot beam, which would allow for comfortable and spacious living quarters.

John was able to purchase the ketch at a very reasonable price, but he had to spend the better part of a year and a great deal of his savings on a complete overhaul of the vessel. When the project was completed in September of 1985, John was delighted with the results. The newly painted and handsomely outfitted old ketch looked and felt like a brand new boat; for John it was a dream come true.

John's first major destination on his leisurely around-the-world journey was Nassau, where he would visit an old friend who had promised to spend some time sailing with him. John intended to use Nassau as a base from which to explore the Bahamian Out Islands during the winter, and then head out for Europe in the spring.

As September is considered the most dangerous month for Caribbean hurricanes, John decided to postpone his departure until the hurricane season had passed, normally the end of October. There is an old West Indian caveat, "September remember, October all over," and John, deferring to conventional wisdom, along with scientifically proven probability models, chose the month of November for the long crossing to Nassau.

With all the major work on the vessel completed, there was no longer any reason to stay at the shipyard in La Guaira, so John took the ketch to Aruba, where he could wait more comfortably. Aruba, like the Caribbean coast of Venezuela, lies south of the hurricane danger zone.

While in Aruba, John began working out at a local health club, an activity that had been his habit for many years. One morning after an aerobics class, John became engaged in a conversation with a beautiful and charming young West Indian woman who attended the club as part of her own daily routine.

The two exercise enthusiasts had other things in common and they soon discovered that they enjoyed each other's company. John took the young lady sailing on the ketch that he had so lovingly rebuilt and she showed John around her native island.

Toward the end of October, John began final preparations for his voyage to Nassau. He topped off the fuel and water tanks, checked and rechecked all systems, equipment and instruments, and did all his last-minute shopping.

On November 1, John's cousin, a business executive on vacation from the stress and hustle-bustle of New York City, arrived in Aruba to accompany him on the sail to Nassau.

Later that week, John said goodbye to his Aruban lady friend and promised to stay in touch. At dawn on the following day, John cast off the lines that connected him and his boat to the land and, along with an eager and enthusiastic crewman, left Aruba behind and headed north, sailing nonstop across the entire width of the Caribbean Sea. They entered the Atlantic Ocean through the Windward Passage, between Haiti and Cuba, and made their first landfall at Great Inagua in the southern Bahamas.

After clearing customs and immigration, John busied himself with the task of re-provisioning the boat, while his cousin instinctively made his way to the nearest telephone to check in with his office. His secretary informed him that something big had indeed come up and that he would have to return to New York as soon as possible. So, just like that, John's one and only crewman packed his gear and left that day on the three-times-a-week Bahamasair flight to Nassau.

His cousin's unexpected departure left John in the position of having to search for another hand to serve as crew before continuing on with the journey. After making several inquiries, John found the perfect candidate: Cecil, a 40-year-old Bahamian who had spent many years working on the *Lady Matilda*, the mailboat that sailed from Nassau to Great Inagua, stopping at Crooked Island, Acklins and Mayaguana.

Just before the scheduled departure, John received a weather report, warning of a tropical storm named Kate that was centered about 100 miles north of the Virgin Islands and moving slowly toward the southwest. The forecast at that time was for gradual strengthening and a track that would take Kate to the south of Great Inagua in about four days.

John had to make a decision.

Great Inagua is low and flat, and offers little-to-no hurricane protection, and to remain at anchor there would mean putting his beloved ketch in grave danger. On the other hand, he could sail to Acklins and Crooked Island, which offered the protection of several different hurricane holes. These islands lay less than a two-day sail to the north. Taking into consideration that Kate was tracking to the south and was more than four days away at its present speed, John decided to make a run for it.

Things did not go as planned. John and Cecil left Great Inagua early in the morning of November 17. John monitored the vessel's position using his state-of-the-art GPS. It soon became apparent that they were not making their expected progress. By late afternoon of the next day, with the vessel now well into the deep Mayaguana Passage, John could clearly see that something was wrong. He checked the compass heading and the boat's speed through the water and both were normal and correct, but they were hardly making any headway at all. John could only come to one chilling realization. The boat was in the grips of a current running in a direction contrary to their destination; and all the while, the weather was deteriorating rapidly.

Meanwhile, Kate was no longer a disorganized tropical storm, slowly moving to the southwest as predicted. She was now a full-fledged hurricane, and unfortunately for John and Cecil, she had picked up her forward speed and had turned to the north, relentlessly tracking straight for the stalled ketch.

And that is how, on the morning of November 19, 1985, John found himself at the helm of a sailboat, far from the sight of land, directly in the path of a class-three hurricane, packing sustained winds of over 120 mph.

The captain of the freighter that John had hailed on the VHF promised to inform the Coast Guard of John's position and to initiate rescue operations. The freighter then disappeared into the storm.

Minutes later, a savage gust tore the reefed staysail from the deck. John called Cecil, who had been resting below decks, and the two men carefully took down what remained of the sails and, using the powerful diesel engine, attempted to keep the bow of the boat pointed into the wind and the waves. The boat kept falling off the wind; heeling over and turning almost broadside to the seas before it would respond to the rudder and once again turn into the wind.

Controlling the boat was made even more difficult by a thick layer of foam that completely covered the surface of the ocean; a foam that not only obscured the view, but also made breathing extremely difficult. It soon became obvious that they could not control the boat, even with the engine running at full throttle. It was too rough, the winds too strong, and the waves too big. They killed the engine, and went into the wheelhouse, battening down the main companionway hatch behind them.

Suddenly the men heard a terrifying roar. An enormous breaking wave engulfed the heeled-over boat and turned it upside down. For a long moment, Cecil and John found themselves floating in the air, as if gravity had ceased to exist. Then they crashed down with a bang into the panels and instruments of the wheelhouse, head first.

John's skull was split open at the forehead, and he sustained an inch-and-a-half-deep gash in his leg. Cecil's nose and right arm were broken. There was blood everywhere.

John panicked and yelled, "That's it! Let's get out of here!"

The ketch was equipped with an unsinkable double-ended 12-foot dory that served as a lifeboat. It had been securely fastened behind the mizzenmast onto heavy-duty ribbed aluminum davits, but when the terrified men were able to get out on deck, all they found were those empty davits, twisted like pretzels by Kate's monstrous waves.

Now more frightened than ever, the men crawled back into the wheelhouse – just in time for another gigantic wave that turned them over once again. The main hatch gave way under the intense pressure and a torrent of water, stronger than ten fire hoses put together, entered the cabin. John and Cecil were once again sent flying.

Two large sofas came loose and one of them pinned John upside down with his head underwater. He held his breath and thought, "...so this is how I'm going to die...."

But John's time was not up yet; the heavy keel sought its lowest level and caused the vessel to complete its 360-degree roll. The sofa shifted its position and freed John from its death grip.

The last roll had knocked down the two masts, leaving a tangle of rigging all over the deck while sections of the heavy mast banged into the boat as the waves battered the hull. With the masts down, the sideways pressure was released and the boat stopped turning over.

That was the good news. The bad news was that every wave flooded into the open hatch and down into the cabin, adding to the four feet of water that had already come in while the boat was upside down. Something had to be done or the boat would sink.

With great effort, John and Cecil managed to close off most of the breached hatch by stuffing in a hastily cut out piece of a mattress. The electric bilge pumps, which should have come on automatically, did not do so. John tried the manual switch and then realized that the entire ship had lost power.

Cecil dragged himself to the engine room to see what he could do. He saw that the batteries, which had been secured by steel cages, had fallen out when the boat had overturned. This explained the failure of the bilge pumps. Moreover, without power, there would be no fresh water to drink and to wash their wounds and no lights to lessen the terror of their situation.

Cecil then tried to get to the manual bilge pump that was also located in the engine room, but the floor was covered with the spilled battery acid, which burned his hands when he tried to crawl in.

The two desperate men then began an almost ridiculously painstaking operation of manual bailing.

The main cabin, which needed to be bailed, was inaccessible because heavy pieces of furniture, floating in water four feet deep, were banging from side to side as the boat rolled and pitched in the heavy seas.

In order to bail the cabin, a bucket had to be lowered by line from the wheelhouse to the cabin below. The bucket, filled with water, was then hauled back up to the wheelhouse. The heavy mattress serving as a makeshift hatch then had to be removed in order for the men to dump out the water, all the while hoping that another wave would not break onto the deck and into the cabin while the hatch was uncovered. The hatch would then be resealed and the operation repeated.

Nonetheless John and Cecil bailed, despite their broken bones, despite their dehydration, despite their loss of blood; they bailed, and they bailed, and they bailed. They were weakened by fatigue and pain and demoralized by the hopelessness of their situation and still they bailed, and they bailed. When the last bits of their strength gave out, sheer determination pushed them to go on. They continued bailing, but the pace turned slower and slower.

At some point in the middle of the dark night they gave up. In the aft cabin was a double bunk that was high enough to be above the level of the water. John and Cecil gave up the ghost. Fully expecting to drown when the water level rose enough to sink the boat, they crawled into the bunk and went to sleep.

It was not their time. Several hours later they awoke and were amazed to see the water still at the same level. Kate had moved on.

Although John and Cecil were no longer in immediate danger of drowning, their lives were still threatened by dehydration and loss of blood. If they weren't rescued soon, they would die.

That afternoon Cecil heard the sound of an engine in the distance. John and Cecil came up on deck and looking up above their crippled vessel, they saw a Coast Guard spotter-plane circling overhead and they knew that the nightmare was over.

AUTHOR'S NOTE:

In 1994 I received a call from John, asking me if I would like to accompany him on a sail between Bocarón, Puerto Rico and Samaná Bay in the Dominican Republic. He was on his way back to Miami after a pleasure cruise through the Caribbean in his new boat, a 45-foot sloop.

During our crossing of the Mona Passage I asked John how he got the big scars on his forehead and leg. It was then that he told me the story of his hurricane experience in 1985.

Also on board for the crossing was John's recent bride, the woman he had met in Aruba and fallen in love with.

MORE NOTES:

THE RESCUE

After the worst of Kate had passed over the stranded sailors, the improving weather conditions allowed the Coast Guard to begin a search-and-rescue mission.

Acting on the information provided by the passing freighter, the Coast Guard sent out a reconnaissance aircraft from their base in Hialeah to search the area where it was calculated that the vessel might be, if it miraculously was still afloat. When the Coast Guard plane spotted John and Cecil, they radioed the nearest ship, which happened to be a large U.S. Naval vessel.

The seas were still incredibly rough and some time was spent formulating a plan of how exactly to accomplish the rescue. Finally a specially trained team aboard a 30-foot diesel-powered liberty launch was able to come alongside the ketch and take aboard the half-dead survivors.

THE RECUPERATION

John and Cecil were treated and stabilized at the ship's infirmary and were taken to the U.S. Naval Base at Guantanamo Bay, Cuba for further treatment.

When they had recovered enough to travel, Cecil was flown back to the Bahamas, where he was admitted to the government hospital in Nassau, and John was brought to Miami, where he would spend the next three months recuperating from the ordeal.

John was left with scars on his forehead and leg. It was a full year before the deep gash on his leg was fully healed.

Cecil's head wound left a deeper imprint, a scar extending from his hairline to halfway down his nose.

KATE

Hurricane Kate made landfall over the Florida Panhandle on November 22, setting a record as the sixth storm to strike the United States mainland that season. Kate was responsible for six deaths and between 250 and 500 million dollars in damages.

THE KETCH

Before allowing himself to be taken aboard the liberty launch, John had obtained a promise from the captain of the Navy ship that the ketch would also be saved. The captain radioed the Coast Guard Base and informed them of the position of the abandoned ketch. The Coast Guard assured the captain and John that a cutter would be sent to tow the vessel back to the nearest base.

Nonetheless, one month later, the Bahamas Defense Force reported finding a boat meeting the description of John's ketch washed up on the sand at Ragged Cay. The vessel had been stripped.

John was still recovering in the Miami hospital when he received the news about his boat's discovery. He asked his friend in Nassau to see what he could do. John's friend ascertained that the ketch in question did, in fact, belong to John. He then chartered a flight to Ragged Cay, where with the help of local fishermen, he was able to get the ketch off the sandbar. The inter-island mailboat, *Emmette and Cephas,* was then enlisted to tow the boat to Nassau.

When asked what he should do next, John instructed his friend to sell the boat. He felt that he had enough for awhile.

The new owners refurbished the vessel once again, and the old steel ketch is still sailing today doing charter work out of Nassau.

A SHARED EXPERIENCE

BY GERALD SINGER

The American Airlines A-300 jumbo jet bound for St. Thomas sat at the beginning of the runway at the John F. Kennedy International Airport waiting for clearance to take off. It was a sunny summer morning and the air above the greater metropolitan area was crystal clear and smog-free.

Sitting in one of the window seats was a six-year-old boy. His father sat beside him and his mother was sitting across the aisle in the four-seat center row of the wide-bodied aircraft. I occupied the seat next to her. Looking out the window where the little boy was sitting I could see the Manhattan skyline in the distance.

In a few minutes the massive Rolls Royce jet engines roared to life, and the aircraft began to move down the runway.

Taking off in an airplane, especially in a jet plane, puts me right in the moment. The awesome power of the jets – that deep steadily increasing sound that gets right inside you – the acceleration, the sensation of speed, faster and faster down the runway – the lift off – the conquering of the very gravity that you've always accepted as being one of the great truths, the gravity that sticks you to the Earth. The freedom of flight! – I'm right there! – I love it!

I look over at the little boy. His face is pressed against the window. His smile tells all. The faster the plane moves, the bigger his smile becomes. When the jet lifts off the ground into the New York sky, he is positively aglow with the excitement of the moment. I know what he is feeling.

Then the boy turns away from the window. He looks over at his mother, catches her eye and then glances at me.

We look back and smile. The moment becomes even more precious. The experience was shared.